HELL ON EARTH

Life of the Dead Book 1

TONY URBAN

PACKANACK
publishing

Join Tony's mailing list & get 3 FREE short horror stories:

http://www.tonyurbanauthor.com/

"For my mother, who shared with me her loves of reading and horror movies and never stopped believing."

The life of the dead is placed in the memory of the living.

— CICERO

I will knock down the Gates of the Netherworld,

I will smash the doorposts, and leave the doors flat down,

and will let the dead go up to eat the living!

And the dead will outnumber the living!

— The Epic of Gilgamesh - 2100 BC

CHAPTER ONE

THE SETTING SUN provided just enough of an orange glow for Wim to see that the streets were clear of zombies. Well, ones up and walking anyway. The bodies of over four dozen men and women littered the small grid of streets that made up his hometown. He'd killed them all.

After the first few, much of the shock wore off, and it was little different than plowing the fields or harvesting the crops. Just another job, albeit a bloody one.

It was time to return to the farm. He could finish this messy work tomorrow or the day after that. He had a feeling time didn't matter much anymore. Still, the day had been long and hot, and he'd worked up quite a thirst. All he had at the farm was prune juice, spoiled milk, and whatever water still remained in the holding tank.

Wim felt it best to gather a few supplies before heading home, and Bender's store was the only choice in town. He knew Old Man Bender wouldn't mind if he raided his little market. He knew Old Man Bender wouldn't mind because he'd put a bullet through his liver-spotted bald head three hours ago. Or was it four? The events of the day had blended together in a bloody, traumatic blur that he didn't care to recollect upon.

When Wim opened the door to the quaint country store—the kind that only still existed in little villages such as this—the first thing he smelled was the rotten meat. Best to avoid the deli and meat counter, he thought.

He grabbed a wobbly shopping card and filled it with cookies and chips and other junk food that would survive a thousand years without perishing. He then took a few jugs of water and added two cases of soda. Not the diet kind, either.

His cart was on the verge of overflowing, and he was ready to turn back toward the exit when thoughts about ice cream overwhelmed him. His brain informed him that if this really was the end of the world and the power was out everywhere, it would also mean the end of ice cream. That was a damned shame as far as he was concerned.

Wim knew the store had a big walk-in freezer in the back. Even though the power had been down for days, the notion that a few tubs of half-frozen ice cream might remain inside — his for the taking and eating — proved too tempting to resist.

Wim strolled to the rear of the store, where he ended up walking by the deli and meat counter after all. He did his best to ignore the flies and maggots, which covered the lunch meats, steaks, pork chops, and other food that would have made his mouth water just days earlier, but he couldn't block out the awful odor.

He found the freezer door closed. That was a good thing, he assumed, because it might have kept most of the cold inside. And preserved the ice cream, of course. He grabbed the silver handle of the freezer, gave it a hard jerk to the right, then pulled. The suction gave way with an audible *pop* as the door opened. A wave of cool-ish air washed over him and his stomach rumbled with hunger. Gosh, he hoped there was chocolate.

He stepped into the freezer, careful to prop the door open with his cart. Four rows of shelving units were stocked full with boxes and goods. On the other side of the room, a few sides of beef hung from a row of meat hooks which dangled from the ceiling.

It seemed, to Wim, an extraordinary amount of merchandise for a small shop in a blink and you'd miss it town, which would make locating the ice cream more complicated than he'd expected. He considered turning back, but the chill in the air and growling in his belly proved irresistible.

Wim checked the first row and came up empty. Row two was a repeat, but in the third, he struck gold. Case after case of ice cream. The good stuff, too, not the generic Tastee! kind he always bought because it was half the price. He pulled down a case of chocolate, and when the box came free, it revealed a zombie on the other side of the shelf.

Wim instantly recognized her as Old Man Bender's wife, a woman he never knew by name, even though he'd seen her at least once a month since he was old enough to stand on his own. Her skin had taken on a blue, almost translucent color, and a thin veneer of ice cloaked her eyeballs. Despite her frozen eyes, she saw Wim, and when she did, her arm shot through the opening in the shelf where the box had been. Her cold, hard hand caught Wim's chin and her fingers scratched and dug into his flesh.

He pushed against the shelf, felt it teeter, then shoved again. It toppled over, raining boxes and cans and buckets down onto the dead woman. She struggled to free herself, and Wim spun away from her. The ice cream was forgotten. All he wanted was to get out.

When he turned, he saw Old Man Bender's two adult sons, their wives, and their three combined children standing between him and the freezer door. All were zombies and all shared the matriarch's cold, blue pallor. They appeared otherwise uninjured except for the oldest man, Doug Bender, who had several bite wounds of various sizes all over his face and arms. Wim could even see his tobacco-stained teeth through a ragged hole in his cheek.

To Wim, it seemed clear what must have happened. The family got sick, then sicker, then started dying. With the town in chaos and no one to help, Old Man Bender must have locked them away in the deep freeze. Only they came back, just like everyone else. Poor Doug must have been the last one alive, and his reward was being the first to feed his newly undead kin. Wim's pondering about the Benders' demise came to a quick halt when the clan staggered toward him.

Wim backed away and tripped over a fallen box. He landed hard, cracking his elbow on the floor, which sent a flash of pain pulsing through his arm. He pushed away the hurt and reached for the pistol holstered at his side, all the while trying to remember how many rounds he'd fired from it and how many he had left. His most optimistic guess was that four bullets remained in the magazine. He found that a disappointingly small number, especially with eight zombies in the freezer with him.

Doug, with his collection of gaping bite wounds, was the closest to him. Wim fired at an upward angle. The bullet zipped through the man's top lip and exploded out the back of his head, painting the ceiling with brains, bone, and coagulated black blood.

Doug collapsed, and Wim aimed the gun at one of the children. The girl was maybe six years old and had her red tresses pulled back in pigtails. She snarled at Wim, baring her bloody teeth and revealing a gap in the front where she'd lost a baby tooth. Wim looked into her dull, milky eyes and shot her in the forehead.

As he prepared to execute one of the Bender wives, cold hands grabbed him from behind, catching handfuls of his hair and jerking him backward. He fell on top of the old matriarch and could feel and smell her chilly, rotten breath on the nape of his neck. Her jaws clicked together, and the sound got closer and closer with every attempted bite. Wim pointed the gun over his shoulder, hoped for the best, and pulled the trigger.

In the initial roar of the gunshot, he thought he might have gone deaf, but soon enough, sound came back into the world in the form of an incessant ringing bell. He felt cold wetness slithering down his neck. When he reached back, he came away with a handful of ripped flesh, pieces of shattered teeth, and clumps of gray hair. Wim dropped the gore and rolled off the now motionless body beneath him.

He got to his feet just in time for another of the children to grab onto his leg. The boy was no more than four or five years old, and Wim kicked out, trying to shake him off. The undead toddler held on like he was going for eight seconds on a bucking bronco. But rather than break loose, the boy darted his head like a snake, striking at Wim's leg. At his crotch. That was too close for comfort, so Wim pressed the barrel of the pistol against the boy's head. When he squeezed the trigger, the gun responded with nothing but a hollow click.

"Well, damn," Wim said, even though no one alive was listening to what he had to say. He wished he had reloaded the pistol before coming into the store. He looked from the undead tot to the other four zombies making their way toward him. "I should have passed on the ice cream."

———

ONE WEEK EARLIER

WIM LOST TRACK OF HOW LONG HE'D BEEN TRYING TO GET AN ACCURATE count on the rats, but he supposed it was at least half an hour. On farms, rats were ordinarily little more than an annoyance. He didn't even bother putting out traps unless they got into the eggs or started nipping at the cow's teats. But this wasn't an ordinary rat or two in the grain or swimming in the shit-filled troughs that funneled the manure out of the barn. This was an abomination.

He saw the thing as soon as he stepped into the barn. The setting sunlight dribbled through the gaps in the wood siding and painted warm, yellow streaks on the dusty floor. At first, he thought it was a pile of rotting, moldy straw. Until it moved.

From where he stood in the bright expanse of the open barn door, the mass of rodents looked to be tied together at their tails. He wondered if some crazy person could have made this thing. Maybe a Boy Scout gone mad after trying for too long to master sheepshanks and bowlines.

As Wim inched closer, it became clear that some tails were indeed knotted, but others were bound by matted hair, woven together into some obscene breathing tapestry. Other rats had physically grown together, the way a tree limb will envelop a power line if they neighbor too close for too long. It made Wim wonder how long this thing had been becoming.

A mischief of rats, Wim thought. He seemed to remember his Pa telling him that's what a group of rats was called. It wasn't as dramatic as a murder of crows, but it somehow felt right.

The heap of filthy gray and brown fur stretched more than three feet across, and once he counted all the way up to thirty-seven, before they moved and he lost track again. The way they moved bothered him the most.

Much of the time they struggled against each other, squealing and shrieking in ratty frustration. But now and again, the whole of the group snapped into a singular mindset and moved as one, skittering about on scores of tiny feet until it stumbled upon some old corn or spilled feed or anything it could gorge on.

As they ate, they fought amongst themselves, biting and chewing on each other. Then he realized some of them weren't moving at all.

Several were nothing more than lifeless husks, bound to the others, to be dragged endlessly to and fro.

One rat sunk its yellow incisors into the face of its nearest neighbor, and Wim saw the flesh peel away to reveal crisp, white bone underneath. The maimed rat squealed and pulled to escape, but its tail was an anchor it was unable to escape.

Other rats, sensing weakness or smelling blood or both, lunged onto their wounded companion and ate it alive. Bright red blood spurted and covered the vermin closest to it. That seemed to enrage them even more, and, soon, the entire writhing mass was on the move again.

Wim tried to remember if he'd ever seen anything on the farm more horrible than this. All that came to mind was a calf that was born when he was six or seven.

Its body was normal, and so was one head. Yet, jutting from the side of its neck like a goiter grew a second malformed skull, which hung lazily to the side as if it was always half asleep. A thick gray tongue lolled from its mouth and slimy drool leaked out near constant, like water from a worn-out faucet.

The eyes on that second head were closed most of the time, but now and again, the lids would flutter and open part way, and underneath they looked alert. The head would raise up a little bit and the eyes would lock on you, and you could almost see it thinking, and that made it all the worse. Wim had asked his Pa why they couldn't cut off that second head, but the old man only shook his.

"Got to put 'em down," Pa said as he looked in the general direction of the freakish calf, but not at it. "It's a portent."

Wim didn't know what a portent was back then, and he wasn't entirely sure now either, but that night he heard a gunshot and never saw the calf and a half again. Later that summer, the crops failed, and they had to sell over eighty head of cattle to keep the mortgage current. The farm never recovered. Neither did Pa.

The old man was pushing seventy, and at six and a half feet tall, he looked like a skinny giant. Even the smallest clothes hung off his frame like from a scarecrow. He'd had another family when he was young, but that broke apart after his first wife died, and Wim only heard about his half-siblings in occasional dribs and drabs. Mama once told Wim that she was halfway to becoming an old maid when his Pa found her. She had long given up notions of being a mother, but God was a trickster, and, at the age of fifty-four, Wim happened.

They were as happy as any given family until that summer when things got dark. Suppers, which had previously been the highlight of their work-filled days, were now eaten in silence. Pa kept his face, with all its harsh angles, turned down toward his food as he shoveled it into his mouth. Wim saw more of the top of his bald head than his eyes, and Mama bustled about the kitchen to avoid the quiet.

When the food was all eaten, Pa would disappear back into the barn. Mama washed the dishes and sometimes remembered to read Wim a story before bed, but most often, she sat by the window and looked to the barn and waited. Wim never worked up the courage to ask her what she was waiting for.

The rats neared the barn door, and, for a moment, Wim was tempted to let them flee. He could let them skedaddle into the field and disappear into the fading light of day and on to another farm where they'd become someone else's problem. But his parents raised him to be responsible, and he couldn't let them down, even years after their deaths.

Instead, he crossed to the wall, where shovels and pitchforks and scythes hung unused, and reached for his Pa's old shotgun, which guarded nothing but rusty junk. He couldn't remember the last time the gun had been touched. When he took it down, he destroyed a heavy canopy of spiderwebs.

Wim pumped a round of buckshot into the chamber and turned back to the mischief of rats which had stopped moving toward the open door, toward freedom, and stared at him.

Do they know what's coming?

An army of black and red eyes watched him as he raised the gun. They didn't make any attempt to flee. Didn't react in any way at all. They only waited. Wim pondered that they had accepted their coming fate, but doubted rats could think about anything beyond their next meal, let alone their mortality. He thought again of the two-headed calf and wondered if they had stared at Pa the same way before he put it down.

Then, Wim squeezed the trigger.

CHAPTER TWO

OVER EIGHT THOUSAND people crowded the streets around City Hall, but all Doc could concentrate on was the overwhelming smell of hot urine that filled the air. He'd been to Philadelphia countless times in his life, but that olfactory assault never ceased to disgust him, and each time he swore he'd never return. At least, now he had a good reason.

The President of the United States stood before the crowd, blathering on with his typical re-election nonsense. Hope. Change. Stop this. Win that. Blah, blah, blah. He mustered up an appropriate amount of zeal and faux sincerity, and the onlookers ate it up like the sheep they were.

Doc harbored no specific grudge against the President. He was another stuffed suit bought and paid for by the banks and corporations—the ones that controlled the country and its leaders regardless of their supposed party. The President was a marionette, contorting when they pulled the strings and speaking canned lines fed to him by his owners. Doc didn't blame the puppet for the puppeteer's manipulations, but he had no respect for the man, either.

His disdain for politics was trumped only by his contempt for the worthless dregs that allowed themselves to be manipulated and misled. Those idiots thought they actually mattered. And thousands upon thousands of the fools stood there in almost hundred-degree heat, gobbling up the President's rhetoric with near frenzied glee.

Doc tuned out the President, ignored the eau de piss, and turned his attention to those nearest to him. A lesbian couple, locked in an embrace, had scrawled the words "Love is" and "never wrong" in black marker on their foreheads. A cadre of protesting senior citizens each held signs reading, "We are the greatest generation!" Some college students with green hair and a plethora of piercings sang America the Beautiful and got most of the words wrong. Doc wished that he could call Guinness to see if this was a record-setting gathering of idiots.

He hated every last one of them. But that was fine because he and he alone would be responsible for their demise.

For the past few days, he'd been sick with worry that something would go wrong. That he'd get stopped by the police for something foolish like jaywalking or forgetting to use a turn signal and his false ID would fail a close inspection. Or that he'd somehow ended up on a watch list, and the large, boot-shaped birthmark on his left cheek would make it all too easy for some overeager Secret Service agent to spot him in the crowd.

He'd spent the entire night prior vomiting into a bucket in the back of his van, and when he looked at himself in the mirror that morning, he saw a man who could pass for a wino or drug addict. Fortunately, that wasn't an unusual sight in the City of Brotherly Love. Two full bottles of Pepto Bismol and a one-dollar razor from the nearby WaWa helped clean up his insides and outsides. When he put on his suit, which was professional-looking but not designer (*Do nothing to stand out*), the transformation was complete.

He looked toward the roof of City Hall and was pleased to see a collection of flags swaying in the wind. It's time, he thought with relief as his patience was exhausted.

Doc reached into the pocket of his pants with his right hand and caressed the cool, smooth glass vials with his fingertips. He rolled them back and forth, enjoying the tinkling sounds they made as they danced together. All of the surrounding nonsense faded away as he popped off the corks with a thumbnail and emptied the contents into his palm.

The President must have said something particularly inspiring because the crowd burst into cheer and threw their hands in the air in celebration. Doc followed their lead and, in doing so, opened his fist and released the almost invisible dust. He felt the gentle breeze caress his cheeks and blow his thin, gray hair askew, and he knew it was done. Sorry, Mr. Eliot, but the world doesn't end with a bang or with a whimper. It ends with a flick of the wrist.

Doc turned his back on the President and worked his way through the army of admirers. Because they were packed together so tight, his retreat took nearly half an hour. That was okay. The pungent smells, the stupidity of the masses, the fear of being caught, it had all ceased to bother him. When he reached the end of the crowd on Broad Street, he glanced back and imagined what was to come and felt gooseflesh pop on his forearms.

"Together, we shall overcome those who stand against us!" the President's voice boomed out over strategically placed loudspeakers. "Together, we will not only survive but thrive!"

"Isn't this... wonderful?"

Doc turned to the source of the labored voice and saw a woman in a wheelchair staring up at him. Her too-small body and the tube running from her throat were telltale signs of muscular dystrophy. She smiled with the kind of dopey optimism and happiness known to children who don't understand the truth or feeble-minded adults who can't think for themselves.

Doc nodded. "Indeed it is."

He saw tears leaking from her eyes as she looked toward the President, who, at this distance, was little more than an ant.

"I don't think... I've ever felt..." She took another gasping breath. "So hopeful."

She reached out to Doc, a gesture that required considerable effort. He knelt down beside her so they were on the same level. Then he took her limp, useless fingers in his death-covered hand and gave them a gentle squeeze.

"Everything is going to be better now," he said.

She smiled again. As she looked from the spec of the President to the man in front of her, her dull, pea soup green eyes found his birthmark. He'd grown used to the stares at the fist-sized, wine-colored blemish but was taken aback when the crippled woman reached out and caressed it.

"God bless you."

"He has. He most certainly has."

Doc left her and continued down the street until he came to the white panel van in which he'd been sleeping for the past three days. "AAA Construction" was stenciled on the side, along with a cartoon gorilla smoking a cigar and wielding a hammer. He unlocked the van, climbed inside, and drove away, leaving the end of the world behind him.

CHAPTER THREE

THE CHICKENS DIED FIRST.

As usual, Wim woke early. Almost an hour before sunrise. He enjoyed the quiet of the predawn when he felt like the only living creature on the farm. It was a special sort of peace.

He had an easy, if numbing, morning routine. He dragged the bedsheets back into place, then covered them with a blue and white log cabin quilt his Mama had sewn by hand. He dressed without giving it much thought as his entire wardrobe consisted of blue jeans and plaid shirts.

With the bed made, he moved on to the bathroom, where he sat on the toilet and gave a small shiver when his bare ass cheeks kissed the cold porcelain. It took considerable effort and a full eight minutes to go, and he wondered if timing his bowel movements was a sign that he was growing old.

As he brushed his teeth, he caught himself staring at his twin in the mirror and tried to see his parents again. He recognized Mama's pitch black hair in the mop atop his head and his Pa's robin's egg blue eyes staring back at him, but the resemblances ended there. Wim had grown used to the crow's feet at the corners of his eyes, but the longer he looked, the more he thought he saw the start of jowls, a sight which distressed him so much he pretended it was only a trick of the light from the bare bulb that hung from the ceiling. He jerked the cord, and the room turned gray.

After his bathroom duties, Wim put a pot of steel cut oats on the stove. As it cooked, he sorted through the fridge, passing by the milk and lemonade and choosing a bottle of prune juice instead. He took a few awful swigs and shoved it back inside.

He stirred the oats as he watched the sun climb over the horizon and turn the barn into a silhouette. It was a clear morning, and the orange star chased away the night. As Wim ate the oats straight from the pot, only pausing a moment to blow cool air on each spoonful, he realized the silence had dragged on a bit too long.

He had four roosters to accompany almost two dozen hens, and one thing he could always count on from the males, aside from being nasty as sin, was their raspy cock-a-doodle-doos welcoming the daylight. But this morning, there were no cocks or doodles or doos. Wim returned the oats to the stove and turned the burner down to warm.

Although the barnyard was bright, the sun had done nothing to heat the air, and Wim regretted not grabbing a jacket. Still due a hard frost, he thought. At least, the cold kept the mud hard.

He circled around the barn to where a thigh-high chicken-wire fence formed the boundaries of the poultry playground. Not a single chicken occupied the fenced-in area. Another bad sign. He lifted away the two-by-four that held the side door shut, set it aside, then pulled the faded red door open.

When he entered the barn, the first sight he saw was forty dead chickens. Scattered about haphazardly, the birds' bodies were clean, not mutilated in any way. That ruled out a stray dog or coyote. Either would have eaten at least a few of them, not simply killed them for fun or sport. Wim crossed to the feathered corpses and knelt down.

He expected to find small, bloody wounds, which would have meant a weasel had gotten inside, killed them, and sucked out the blood. Only there were no wounds on the first bird he checked. Or the second or the third. Wim didn't bother examining a fourth.

He grabbed a wheelbarrow and filled it with the dead chickens. The mound of carcasses heaped so high he thought it might be top heavy and tip as he maneuvered it out of the barn, but he made it. He pushed them to the far end of the barnyard, where he burned his garbage and added them to the ash pile. After retrieving a red jug of gasoline from the barn, he poured a bit onto the mound and set them ablaze. Black smoke filled the air, and the acrid smell made his eyes water. At least, he told himself, it was the smell.

———

LATER THAT AFTERNOON, AS WISPS OF SOUR SMOKE STILL DANCED UP from the burn pile, Wim saw that the big sow he unoriginally referred to as Miss Piggy had collapsed on her side near the feed trough. Her breathing was shallow and her eyes closed. He rubbed his palm over her bristly skin.

"What happened to you, old girl?"

Miss Piggy didn't stir. Wim gently pushed up her eyelid and revealed an orb marred by crisscrosses of blood-red veins. Her iris had rolled too far back to be visible. He then pinched her lip between his thumb and forefinger and lifted. The sow's skin peeled loose from her teeth like Velcro, and inside her mouth was no saliva, only dried blood.

Her skin was heavy and malleable like clay and stayed pushed up, even when he pulled his hand away. Wim took care to mold her mouth back into shape, then stroked her ear. She remained unresponsive, so he left her to check on the other three swine. Wim found them dead in the pigpen. He didn't know what had brought this horror to his little farm, but dread filled him up inside like an overfull water pitcher.

Wim rang for the veterinarian on the rotary phone, which hung on the kitchen wall. Each return of the wheel seemed an eternity, and the line rang eight times before a harried answer came.

"Yes!" It was more an exclamation than a greeting.

"Doctor Allen? This is Wim Wagner."

"Oh. Hello, Wim."

"Something's wrong here. This morning, my entire flock of chickens was dead. I just added three more pigs to the list, and the fourth don't look far behind."

"You're a latecomer to that party, Wim."

"Excuse me?"

"I'm sorry. I don't intend to be short with you, but it's the same all over the county. I returned from the McAndrews' farm no more than ten minutes ago. They lost over ninety head of cattle just like that."

Wim heard the doc's fingers snap through the earpiece. "What's going on?"

"If I knew, I'd be in a hell of a lot better frame of mind."

Wim paused, unsure what, if anything, to say.

"Listen. I'll try to stop over this evening, and if not then, tomorrow morning. What do you have left over there?" Doctor Allen asked.

Wim tallied his stock in his head. "Five goats. Three cows. And Miss— one pig."

"Mmm hmm. Well, try to segregate the animals from each other. Do that and hold down the fort until I get there. All right?"

"Yessir, I will."

"And Wim?"

"Yes?"

"You've got to put that sick pig down. I don't know if it's possible to stay ahead of this mess, but that's the only chance."

The call clicked off without a goodbye from the good doctor. Wim held onto the phone for a few long moments before he accepted the fact that better news wasn't coming.

He moved to a place in the house he seldom visited, his Pa's old workroom. The first thing he noticed when he turned on the light were the tools the old man had used to tie flies. Small vises and hooks and bobbins with brightly colored threads. Pliers so small Wim doubted they'd be usable in his own meaty paws.

He didn't know if it was his imagination, but he thought he could still smell the Beech Nut tobacco Pa chewed almost nonstop. That, mixed with the aroma of Hoppes gun oil, was the old man's cologne. Hung on the back wall of the room were a variety of rifles and revolvers. On the sprawling oak desk his Pa had built all on his own was box upon box of ammunition. Wim ignored all the firearms and reached into a drawer to grab a different type of gun.

The captive bolt pistol had been used only twice before. It was quick and efficient, like it was designed to be, but Wim thought it made doling out death obscenely easy. And as he shuffled across the barnyard toward his dying pig, he worried that she deserved a less mechanical ending.

She hadn't moved since he last saw her and her breaths came in shallow, hitching wheezes. He knelt before her and traced his fingers over her belly, gently scratching like she'd so enjoyed before this whole mess. She remained unresponsive. Wim leaned into her and whispered in her ear.

"I'm real sorry about this, Miss. You were a good mama and a good pig."

He pressed the barrel of the gun against the center of her forehead. When he pulled the trigger, a stainless steel bolt shot out with a *boom*, broke through her skull, destroyed her brain, then retreated back into the pistol with a *swish*. The entire process took a fraction of a second.

Wim followed the vet's instructions and quarantined the rest of the animals from one another.

It didn't help. By sunset, the doctor had failed to show, and every animal on the farm was dead.

CHAPTER FOUR

In May of her eighteenth year, Ramey Younkin lost her virginity, failed her senior year of high school, and watched the world as she knew it come to an end. In many ways, the awkward and painful two minutes in the back of Bobby Mack's Ford Tempo was the worst part. God, he was such a white trash loser.

Life had been a consistent downward spiral since her father left them two years earlier. Not that she blamed him. Loretta, his wife and Ramey's mother, was almost a decade into a drug addiction, which started with pain pills after a minor back injury. When the local pain clinics caught on to her game, she moved on to trading prescription narcotics with her minivan mom friends the same way little boys swap baseball cards.

When her father left, he asked—more like begged—Ramey to join him. But she was one of the cool girls in her sophomore high school class and actually enjoyed living in the town she now realized to be nothing more than a dead-end wasteland of unemployment and welfare. The sort of place people only lived because they had young children to raise or old parents to look after. Or because they were too stupid to realize how awful it was. She also knew that if left all alone, her mother would be dead in no short order. So, Ramey stayed.

A year ago, Ramey woke to a 4 a.m. phone call. After taking twenty dollars for a happy ending at the truck stop by the turnpike, Loretta's would-be John turned out to be an undercover cop who arrested her for prostitution.

Rather than go down quietly, she fought with the officer, scratching his eye so bad he needed surgery. Loretta was also high as a kite on oxy, a drug for which she had no prescription. That hat trick earned her three months in the county jail and a fine so hefty they had to sell the house Ramey grew up in.

That's how they ended up in a thirty-five-year-old double-wide in the Happy Acres Mobile Home Park. And that's how Ramey went from being elected to the homecoming court to daily catcalls and insults every time she strolled down the school hallway.

At first, she thought the taunting would end if she ignored it. It didn't. She skipped a day here or there when she didn't feel up to the harassment, then skipped entire weeks. When May rolled around, a letter came in the mail, stating that she had missed forty-five days and had been expelled. Apparently, the maximum number of days you could miss and still graduate was forty. If she'd known that fact, she would have kept count.

The day she received the letter was the day Bobby Mack told her she looked beautiful in green when she passed him at the community mailboxes. He probably meant her tits looked good in the tight, "Kiss Me I'm Irish" (she was not) t-shirt she was wearing, but at her lowest of lows, she took the bait. Ten minutes later, they were sharing a joint in his car. Fifteen minutes after that, he had her jean shorts off. Two minutes later, she realized flunking out of high school a month before graduation wasn't the worst part of her day after all.

Bobby kept sniffing around like a randy dog, but one mistake was enough for Ramey, and every time she saw him around the trailer court, she spun and raced the other way. She vowed to get back on track and enrolled in cyber schooling. It was all going according to plan for about a week.

Loretta threw open the metal screen door of the trailer. Because the hydraulic stopper was missing, it swung all the way out and crashed into the cheap aluminum siding. Ramey, in the middle of a calc test on her laptop, barely looked up. Nothing about her mother was subtle, not even her entrances.

"Hi, Mom."

"Morning, Babe."

"It's almost three in the afternoon."

"Thaswha Imeant."

Her eyelids drooped, and she looked two decades older than her forty years. She was pretty once, in a small town trashy sort of way with her permed dishwater blonde hair and curvy figure. With a little maintenance, she could have been beautiful. But drugs had taken away her looks, just like they had taken her husband, her home, her job, and her future. Her eyes sat deep in skeletal sockets, and when she opened her mouth, she revealed a set of teeth that would scare away small children. Ramey still hadn't grown accustomed to her mother's new look.

"Sure you did," Ramey said without looking up from the computer.

"Don't sass me, smarmouth."

Loretta stumbled into the cabinet holding their mismatched yard sale dishes. After paying her fines and buying this rundown trailer, almost all the money from the sale of the house evaporated. Aside from a few thousand dollars that Ramey had hidden for a rainy day (she had a feeling a monsoon was coming), Loretta burned through the rest in months.

With the stigma of her arrest, Loretta's minivan mom friends turned their backs on her. After all, they only popped pills recreationally, they weren't dirty whores. With her oxy supply cut off, Loretta turned to heroin. The sores and track marks on her arms gave that away, and Ramey wasn't believing her affirmations that they were mosquito bites or poison ivy, depending on which lie her mother felt like telling that particular day. She'd given up on trying to save her mom. It was hard enough trying to save herself.

Loretta took an Old Milwaukee from the fridge and collapsed onto their stained floral print couch. She turned on the old tube TV, possibly the only such television remaining in America, Ramey thought and flipped through the channels.

Ramey heard a reporter say, "Vice President has been sworn," before the station changed. Loretta settled on a faux reality show where camo-clad hillbillies discussed the merits of jerky made from venison versus jerky made from beef. In the midst of their argument, the oldest of the men broke wind. and Loretta laughed so hard she, too, farted one so loud and wet that if she'd been sober, she might have checked her underwear just to be on the safe side. But sober she was not, so her own fart only made her cackle even more. The laughter quickly dissolved into a violent coughing fit, which she drowned out with the beer.

Ramey tried to tune it all out and concentrate on antiderivatives and integrals. By the time she finished her test, Loretta was passed out on the couch and snoring like a buzz saw. Ramey realized the television had gone silent. At first, she assumed their service had been shut off due to an unpaid bill. But when she looked at the screen, she saw a generic announcement reading, "This is a Test of the Emergency Broadcasting System. This is only a Test." Ramey scrolled through the channels and saw they all had the same white text on the same blue background.

She shut off the TV and returned her attention to the laptop. A quick trip to Twitter seemed normal enough at first. #EastWestKardashian-Baby was the top hashtag, but second on the list was #deadpresident.

Further down, after #beiberpenis and #beyonceshair was even stranger.

#zombiepresident

Ramey clicked away from Twitter for an actual news site, but before one could load, the Internet went down.

CHAPTER FIVE

As he snorted a thin line of coke off the fifteen-year-old girl's perky C-cup breast, Mitch realized his life was damned near perfect. Months ago, if you'd have told him he would love private school, he'd have said you were a stupid son of a bitch. He'd assumed the kids would all be nerdy little rich fuckers who wanted to be surgeons or physicists or, like his own father, politicians.

The rich fuckers part was right, of course. Only God and his father knew how much tuition here was, but that was his only correct assumption. For the most part, his fellow classmates were just like him. Kids with too much money, too little responsibility, and parents who were too busy to supervise. Or care, for that matter. Mitch was days away from finishing his junior year at The Marsten Academy and never wanted it to end. Especially with Rochelle's perfect, bouncy tits to play with.

"Save some for me, Mitchy," she said as he made another line disappear up his nose. "Don't hog it."

He grabbed a glass vial and considered pouring the cocaine on his cock but settled on the back of his hand. Rochelle quickly sniffed it away. Mitch watched as her pupils contracted and her IQ dropped to double digits and he grinned. A hyena's grin. He poured more coke on the tip of his tongue, then took her perfect, pencil eraser sized nipple into his mouth and rolled his drug-laced tongue around it. She moaned so loud and long he thought he might cum just listening to her.

They fucked like rabbits. When she was high, she'd do anything Mitch could imagine and some things he'd never even seen on the internet. God, he'd been so very wrong about private school.

Rochelle passed out after almost an hour of screwing, but Mitch was flying high, and sleep was nowhere on his horizon. He grabbed his cell phone and saw he had eight missed calls, all from the same caller—Senator SOB according to his caller ID—otherwise known as his father. He thought about listening to the eight subsequent voicemails, then decided against it. The day was going great, why ruin it?

Instead, Mitch took a bottle of Valium (prescribed to one Rosalita Guiterrez) from the nightstand and popped two in his mouth. He was halfway through dry swallowing them when the phone rang again.

"Son of a bitch!" As the words came out of his mouth, a pill snagged in his throat. He coughed and gagged as the bitter taste filled his mouth. When the pill finally slid down his gullet, he swiped the phone to answer. When he tried to speak, his raw throat spasmed, and another coughing fit overcame him.

"Mitchell? Are you sick? What's wrong?"

Mitch found an almost empty can of Red Bull on the floor and downed the few remaining sips of liquid. "I'm fine. What do you want?"

"Didn't you get my messages?"

"I was studying," Mitch said as he looked at the beautiful, naked girl on his bed. "Anatomy." He had to cover the phone as he laughed at his own joke.

"Forget about that."

That was new. Senator SOB was all about studying. Mitch realized something must be seriously wrong and wondered if he'd done something worthy of expulsion. Maybe his side business dealing drugs had been exposed. As he thought about round two with Rochelle, he hoped that wasn't the case.

"You're being evacuated."

"What?"

"I've sent a helicopter for you. It will arrive within the hour."

"What?"

"You're a spoiled asshole, Mitchell, but you're not stupid, so open your ears and close your mouth. There is a viral outbreak and Congress and their families are being moved to a safe zone. Go to the football field and wait. Don't take anything with you. And speak of this to no one."

Mitch wanted to say 'what' again but stopped himself. He hated his father, but what he heard in the man's voice differed from the anger and rage he often aimed in Mitch's direction. What he was hearing was fear.

"Yes, sir." He hadn't called his father sir in years, if ever.

The line went dead.

———

MITCH STOOD ON THE 50-YARD LINE WHEN HE HEARD THE HELICOPTER approaching from the south. He'd left Rochelle asleep in the bed. That was easier than trying to explain away a last minute chopper ride to who the fuck knows where, especially when he was forbidden to give out any details.

A viral outbreak, his father had said. What did that even mean? Zika? Ebola? It must be pretty fucking serious to round up everyone in Congress and their dipshit families. He wondered if that was just a cover story and if the truth was an impending terrorist attack. Maybe ISIS had bought a fleet of nukes and was planning to make every major U.S. city glow.

When he saw that the chopper dropping from the sky was of the military variety, his terrorist theory gained even more strength. A door swung open and a soldier carrying one of the biggest rifles Mitch had ever seen pointed at him.

"Mitchell Frederick Chapman?"

Mitch nodded. His mouth had gone too dry to speak.

"Show me your ID."

Not even a please. Mitch flashed the Student ID on his lanyard. The soldier examined it, looked at Mitch's face, then turned his attention to a clipboard. He saw what he wanted and waved Mitch forward. When he was close enough, the man grabbed Mitch by the back of the jacket and hoisted him aboard. Mitch fell into the dusty canvas seat and rolled into a sitting position.

"Buckle up."

Mitch saw the soldier's nameplate read Miller and did as ordered. "Where are we going?"

Miller didn't respond to Mitch. Instead, he hammered the cockpit door, and the helicopter began a rapid ascension. Mitch looked down at the campus, where a few of his classmates were looking skyward toward the spectacle.

"Hey, where are you taking me?"

The soldier looked at Mitch through his black sunglasses. "That's classified. Speaking of which, let me see your phone."

It took Mitch two tries to pull it from his pocket because his hands had gone cold and sweaty. He handed it over to Miller, who immediately powered the unit down. Mitch held out his hand for its return, but Miller tossed it out of the chopper, where it plummeted into the abyss.

"Nice," Mitch said. "Thanks for that. You know who my father is, right?" Ugh, the 'you know who my dad is' card. That was low, even for him.

"I do. Now, why don't you shut your ratty little face—" Miller sneezed twice, then resumed, "And be thankful you're one of the few people who get to live through this."

He turned his back to Mitch, who felt like he'd just been punched in the gut. It wasn't the insult. He'd heard worse, even from his own parents.

One of the few people who get to live... What the fuck was happening?

CHAPTER SIX

THE COLD STEEL of the crescent wrench felt good in his hand. He liked the weight of it. That the bolt holding on the broken wheel bearing refusing to budge hadn't even annoyed him. Yet. Solomon Baldwin was a patient man. Patience was, he thought, one of his best qualities. The ability to remain calm when a lesser man would lose his temper or dissolve into a blubbering mess had risen him far beyond his expected station in life.

He clenched his jaw and used almost all of his considerable strength against the bolt. Just as it gave way, he heard two bints chattering away from the sidewalk. One power walked and held small weights in each hand. The other pushed a baby buggy.

Solomon didn't know their names, but their plain homely faces were familiar enough. He remembered them from the neighborhood picnics his wife, Wendy, forced him to attend, even though he'd have rather spent his time crushing his own balls in a vice than socialize. Their voices were murmurs, but he knew they were talking about him.

"Last week, LuAnn saw the guy from the gas company, the one with the beard who reads the meters—"

"He looks like the guy from the *Dos Equis* commercials."

"I guess, kinda. But she saw him walking out of their house," she nodded toward the Baldwin homestead, "zipping up his pants and grinning like a tomcat."

"God, I hope that's true. Maybe I have a chance."

"But your husband's sorta handsome. Not like him." She glanced toward Solomon's driveway but couldn't see him peering back from the cover of darkness beneath the car. "Could you blame her? He reminds me of a wild dog. About as charming as one, too."

"Ever get a good look at his teeth? They look like rotten kernels of corn."

Solomon clenched his fists, and, in doing so, the wrench slipped, and he slammed his knuckles into the undercarriage, ripping the flesh away from the bone. He stayed quiet, though. He wouldn't let those cows know they'd gotten under his skin.

The blood dripped off his hand and splashed against his face in fat, ruby-colored raindrops. Its metallic flavor lit up his taste buds as it streamed into his mouth and across his teeth, which were not unlike rotten corn at all, truth be told.

Solomon Baldwin wasn't big on mottos or slogans or sayings, but if he had to choose a few words to live by, "Just because you're paranoid doesn't mean they aren't out to get you," would have been a good start. That was especially true the last few months.

He'd long suspected his wife was cheating on him again. She dyed her hair bleach blonde and lost half a stone or more. But it was more than that. It was her demeanor. The bird glowed, and she hadn't glowed like that in years.

Proving it was another matter. He'd hired on extra employees at his construction firm, only going out when he needed to bid jobs or meet with clients, all so he could spend more time at home. Only that didn't work. She went out more.

He offered to tag along on her little errands. "It'll be like we're dating again," he assured her, but she wouldn't hear it. "I'm going tanning," was the common excuse. The bird should well be the color of a Hershey bar for as much time as she professed to be spending in tanning beds. But he'd never let on that he suspected anything. He wanted proof before he acted.

Now, it seemed he'd gotten his proof from two busybody neighbors, and there'd be hell to pay. Growing up in Birmingham, the other lads called him Sol. At least, that's what most people assumed. Sol, short for Solomon. Only they weren't really calling him Sol. His nickname was Saw. And he wasn't afraid to use his teeth.

He wiped the blood away from his mouth with the back of his uninjured hand and, in the process, smeared red across the bottom half of his face. He could feel the hot wetness of it against his skin as he slid on his back across the rough pavement and into the light of day. He rolled onto his belly, then raised up on his knees. The gossipy bitches couldn't help but look.

Solomon never lost eye contact with them as he rose to his feet. "Wotcha."

The women looked at each other, eyes narrowed, and Solomon thought they looked like rabbits ready to run from a hungry fox.

"Excuse me?" the uglier of the two asked.

"I'm sorry, ladies. It's the Brummie slipping out of me." He strolled toward them, every step full of purpose. "Just a way of saying 'howdy' back home."

When he reached them, he had to battle back a grin when both took a step away. Solomon was as wide as the two of them put together but only an inch or two taller. What he lacked in height, he made up in power.

"Oh. Well, hello to you, too, Mr. Baldwin."

He gave a broad smile that showed almost all of his remaining teeth. "Fine day out, is it not?"

The less ugly of the two nodded and gave a nervous titter. "It sure is. A good day to do some repairs. And cheaper than going to a mechanic, right?" she said with a motion toward his car.

Solomon looked from the women to the car, then back again. "If I do the work, I know it's done right. Don't have nothing to do with money at all. I got plenty o dat. Or have you heard otherwise?"

She lost her fake smile and glanced at her friend (*help me!*), who remained closed-mouthed. "No, I... I didn't mean that at all. I just meant that garages are so overpriced. You know?"

"I know. Course, I know. Be a fool not to. Do you think I'm a fool?" He could almost feel the fear coming off their bodies like electricity from power lines, and it made him happier than he'd been in weeks.

He knew they were ready to flee, but he wanted to draw the fun out a bit longer, so he looked at the cooing brat buckled into the buggy. The boy was about a year old with a fat face and pallid skin. Drool dribbled from his mouth, and Solomon saw white bits poking from his pink gums.

"Looks like he's gettin his tuttie pegs already."

The women exchanged another confused and fearful glance. "His what?" the mother asked.

He reached down with his blood and grease-stained hand and pushed the toddler's upper lip to show the teeth. "Tuttie pegs. Baby teeth, I guess you birds call them."

"Oh, yes. He's teething almost nonstop lately."

Solomon drew back his hand and left behind a smear of black and red on the boy's small, pinched face. The mother looked down with dismay and extracted a wet nap from her pocket. When she went to use it, Solomon grabbed her wrist.

"He'll be aw right. Little blood and grease is just what a boy needs." He increased the pressure of his grip but exerted far less force than he was capable of producing. "Makes a man out of im."

He released her hand. A white outline remained behind as she drew back, dropping the wet nap to the sidewalk.

"I'll get that for you. Wouldn't want to leave trash lyin around in this fine neighborhood."

As he bent at the waist to pick up the napkin, the two women jumped forward like someone had shot off a starter's pistol. "Thank you, Mr. Baldwin."

"Don't mention it. And call me Saw. All my friends do."

He watched them scurry down the street like the scared rabbits they were. As they disappeared around the corner, he thought to check his watch. His wife should have been home an hour ago. But that was okay. He'd be waiting for her.

CHAPTER SEVEN

ALMOST EVERYONE THOUGHT it was the cities that were cesspools overflowing with assholes with no morals or human decency, but wannabe Mayberrys like the pissant town in which Aben currently found himself were much worse.

Growing up, he'd always heard about small-town values, but in real life, when you are an outsider passing through their borders, their arms are never open and their welcome never warm. That's why he found himself handcuffed to a lead pipe inside what was possibly the smallest police station in the U.S.

He'd arrived in town the night before. A long-haul trucker on route to Kansas City picked him up in Boston, where he'd been panhandling outside a Whole Foods. Aben wasn't looking for a ride, but he'd been rambling around Massachusetts for seven or ten days and was short on cash. New England was pretty but so damned expensive.

The trucker, Jay or Ray—Aben couldn't remember which—was a talker, and during the eight or so hours they spent rolling along the East Coast highways, Aben heard the man's life story backward and forward. Jay or Ray didn't listen much, but that suited Aben fine as he didn't care to be heard.

Crudely cut out pictures from skin magazines filled the cab. Jay or Ray seemed to have a particular fetish for assholes, and several perversely close-up clippings decorated the dash. During the long ride, Aben came to view them as an obscene version of connect the dots. One time, he made a spaceship.

Jay or Ray was a gargantuan man who wore a button-down shirt that was at least two sizes too small. Aben kept waiting for the buttons, which were under constant duress, to pop off like tiny round missiles. He was afraid one might put his eye out. The worry kept him awake the entire trip.

Three-fourths of the way through Pennsylvania, an accident forced them off the turnpike and onto narrow two-lane roads. Jay or Ray, who had been perfectly pleasant until that point, grew increasingly sullen with each laborious mile.

His mood turned even darker when he almost steamrolled a whitetail deer that bounced in front of the truck as the eighteen-wheeler rolled down a steep hill, forcing Jay or Ray to slam on the brakes and come to a squealing stop, which sent the trailer skidding dangerously to the side before the trucker got it back under control.

"Cocksuckersonofabitchfuck!" Jay or Ray blurted out with enough vehemence to send spittle flying into the windshield.

Aben laughed. That was a poor decision because as soon as they hit the next town, Jay or Ray said it was best to part ways. His cab was a dictatorship, and it was not up for debate.

As far as Aben could tell, the town where the trucker had abandoned him consisted of one gas station, a blinking yellow light, and a pizza shop, which sat between a few shuttered storefronts. He decided he was in the mood for Italian and ventured inside.

A purple-haired teenage girl with so much acne on her face she could have been the before picture in a Proactiv ad, leaned on the counter. She half glanced up from her cell phone, then took a better look when she realized the customer was a stranger.

In fairness, Aben understood he didn't make the best first impression. His clothes had gone unwashed for several weeks and his body for almost as long. He had a wild, patchy beard that stretched high onto his cheekbones and made him look more like a werewolf with mange than Grizzly Adams.

"Can I help you?" she asked.

Aben scanned the menu above her head. "I'll take two slices of pie and a Dr. Pepper."

She chewed the inside of her lip, her eyes turned down to the counter to avoid his face. "Umm… We don't got no pie."

Aben examined her. Her vacant, bovine expression confirmed she wasn't cracking wise.

"Pizza will be fine. Two slices, please."

She punched the cash register. "$5.30."

Aben reached into his pocket and pulled out a wad of ones. He peeled off six and extended them to her. She took them with her fingertips and deposited them into the register. She dropped his change on the counter rather than put it in his open palm.

"Be a couple a minutes."

Aben turned toward the seating area, which was free of other patrons. He slid into a grimy booth and stared out at the empty street while he waited. In the time that passed, not a single car drove by. Happening town, that was for certain.

Aben looked around for a jukebox. It seemed like the type of place that would have one, but it did not. The overhead fluorescent lights did little to brighten the restaurant. But if the sticky laminate table was any indication, that was for the best. Numerous chips and deep gouges marred the linoleum tile on the floor and the floor itself was long overdue for mopping. Heck, forget mopping; it needed a hazmat team.

Pizza-face brought his slices and soda, then waited until he looked up at her.

"We're gettin' ready to close."

"It's not even seven o'clock. What time do you close?"

"Soon."

"Can I at least eat first?"

She spun on her heels and stomped away. Good old small-town hospitality.

The slices of pizza were big and greasy but bland. Not enough sauce and too much generic mozzarella. Aben had to wash down the thick, under-cooked crust with his Dr. Pepper, which itself was watery and flat.

He'd barely choked down the first piece when the girl called out from the counter. "Can you go, now?"

Aben ignored her and chomped on piece number two. Before he could finish it, flashing blue lights appeared in the plate-glass window. Of all the shitty towns to get dropped in.

The door opened and a stout, mustachioed cop wearing a generic police uniform and a hat two sizes too large for his tiny head strolled in. Pizza-face pointed at Aben, then the cop walked over and sat down across from him.

"Mind if I have a seat?"

"You already did, Chief," Aben said. Once upon a time, he'd had better control of his mouth, especially around authority figures, but that skill had long since dissipated.

"Suppose that's true."

The cop flashed a toothy grin, revealing teeth so white and perfect they could only be dentures. He didn't look to be out of his forties, and Aben wondered if his tooth loss was due to poor dental health or if someone had knocked the real ones out. Please be the latter, he thought.

"I'm Officer Dolan. And we've got a complaint against you for loitering."

"Not loitering. Eating," Aben said and took another bite of the crappy pizza to prove his point. "And this is a restaurant. Albeit a sad excuse for one."

"I'm going to need to see some ID."

"Don't have any."

"You don't have ID?"

"I do not."

"No driver's license?"

"Don't drive."

"What about a picture ID to do your banking? I mean, how do you cash checks?"

Aben looked at the Podunk piece of shit and thought he might be one of the stupidest men he'd ever met. "Do I look like I get a lot of checks, Chief?"

Dolan's fake smile vanished. "Stand up."

"I'm just trying to eat the food I paid for. I'm not breaking any damned laws."

Dolan shoved the paper plate containing the remnants of the cardboard pizza onto the grimy floor.

"Up. Now, asshole."

Aben sighed and stood.

"Put your hands behind your back."

Again, he obliged. Officer Dolan slapped a pair of metal handcuffs onto him as tight as they would go. How bush league. They don't even use zip ties.

Dolan steered Aben past the counter, where pizza-face watched, smug and satisfied. "Thank you so much! I've never been so scared of no one before."

"Nothing to worry your pretty, little head over, Susie. I've got this under control."

She smiled for the first time all evening and batted her glued-on, fake eyelashes at the officer like he was some kind of matinee idol.

Aben knew better, but he couldn't help himself. He looked her right in the eyes. "Miss, I highly recommend you take that six dollars I gave you and buy yourself some Noxzema."

Then Aben laughed and laughed. Until Dolan slammed his face into the metal door frame.

WHEN ABEN CAME TO, HE WAS SITTING ON THE TOILET. THE FIRST SITE he saw was the top of Officer Asshole's balding head as he sat behind an industrial green metal desk, filling out paperwork. When Aben attempted to stand, his left hand caught on the water pipe going into the bottom of the holding tank, and the unexpected snag jerked him back onto the seat.

Dolan looked up with a sneer. "Have yourself a nice nap?"

With his free right hand, Aben rubbed the goose-egg on his forehead.

"Got some aspirin if you want some."

"I'm good," Aben said as he glanced around the small room and saw it was just the two of them. The cop was shorter than him and much thicker around the middle, but he must be a strong prick if he dragged him around solo.

Dolan tapped his paperwork with his index finger. "You'd be even better if you'd cooperate with me."

Aben examined Dolan up and down and determined he was most likely a local high school hero twenty years removed and gone to seed. He stayed silent.

"Just tell me your damned name. I'll run you through the system, and so long as you don't have any warrants, we'll get you out of here with nothing but a fine," Dolan said.

Aben tilted his head back and stared at the drop tile ceiling. "I have done nothing wrong."

"That's what you keep saying, but if that's so, tell me—" He coughed so hard his torso seemed to spasm. He got out, "Who the fuck," before hacking away again.

Dolan bent at the waist and coughed a good half a minute, his face turning scarlet. Maybe he'll stroke out, Aben thought, and his lips turned up in a small smile. But it passed, and Dolan caught his breath. He pulled out a handkerchief and hocked a thick wad of mucous into the white folds. He examined the goo for a moment, then returned the cloth to his pocket.

"Whew. That one was intense," Dolan said.

Aben recalled a truck stop diner he'd stopped at with Jay or Ray earlier that day. Seemed like everyone was coughing or sneezing, even the waitress who served him his turkey on rye. She'd hacked all over his sandwich, but at least she didn't call the cops on him.

Dolan took a few moments to catch his breath. Then he grabbed his keys and flicked off the lamp on his desk.

"Enough of this shit. If you aren't going to cooperate, you and your smelly ass can sit here alone till the morning." He stood and headed to the door. "The relief officer comes on at seven. After that, one of us will take you to the county lockup."

Aben noticed the clock on the wall showed it was only a few minutes past eight.

"You can't leave me handcuffed to the damned toilet for eleven hours."

"I'll do whatever the fuck I want as long as you want to remain the man with no name."

"What if I need a drink?"

Dolan laughed and coughed at the same time. "Toilet's right under you. Don't know how clean it is. I've never been much for housekeeping, but it's wet."

He flicked off the overhead light when he left. Aben waited for his eyes to adjust to the few remnants of daylight that drifted through the room's only window. He licked his lips and thought they seemed dry all of a sudden. It was going to be a long night.

CHAPTER EIGHT

IT ALL HAPPENED TOO FAST. We never had a chance, Jorge Bolivar thought as he surveyed the pandemonium on the streets.

It had been only three days since his unit had received reports of the outbreak. The army trucked them from North Carolina to Philadelphia, which everyone was referring to as "the hot zone." Their orders were to quarantine the city to control an outbreak of a new strain of the flu, and maybe that was true in the beginning. When their boots hit the pavement, though, it was clear this wasn't the flu. At least not the flu like he, or anyone else, had seen before.

They collected truckloads of dead animals— rats and birds and cats and dogs—and hauled them away to be incinerated. It hit the people soon after. It started with typical cold symptoms, a wet cough and runny nose, then progressed to some type of fever-induced delirium.

The docs said it was a form of encephalitis that fried the brain, and none of the normal drugs had any effect. Once someone was sick, they kept getting worse for a day or two, and then they died.

They didn't stay dead, either. Jorge discovered that morbid fact first-hand when, just minutes after praying with a dying woman in the makeshift field hospital that now occupied the Eagles' football stadium, she awoke from her eternal slumber and tried to bite a nurse who was removing the oxygen mask from her face.

The dead woman's jaws snapped so hard that her dentures shattered. Soldiers quickly strapped her to the bed, and the docs in charge examined her, but she gave off no vitals. They muzzled her like a vicious dog and shipped her away to God knows where.

When the sick died of the disease, they came back like slow and clumsy cannibals. That was bad enough, but Jorge also saw what happened when they managed to bite someone. The first time he saw it happen was when a private, fresh out of high school, got chomped by one of the zombies.

They had orders not to call them that—zombies—but that's what they were. Calling them infected or diseased or whatever other words the brass deemed media friendly and less likely to cause a panic didn't change anything.

The private—his name was Keller, Bolivar thought he recalled—was dragging a lifeless body off the street when, out of nowhere, it reanimated. It bit down on the boy's forearm and ripped right through his U.S. flag tattoo. Bright red arterial blood sprayed from the wound, and the private moved to cover it and stop the bleeding. Within minutes, the life left his eyes. He scrambled about like a crazed animal, every bit as quick as he'd been in life.

The boy made a mad dash toward his fellow soldiers, who gunned him down before he could reach them. The first shots in his chest seemed to have little effect, but the bullet that took off the top of his skull sent him to the ground. He didn't get up.

Complicating matters was that it wasn't always the same. Sometimes, a person turned within seconds of being bitten. Sometimes, they lasted a few minutes, long enough to build up a false sense of hope. The docs speculated that it depended on the person's immune system or perhaps the location of the bite itself. Either way, the unpredictability made the fight even harder.

They stayed ahead of it for about a day, and the outlook was cautiously optimistic. And then it turned. It seemed like all the soldiers got sick at once. Don Rando, a beefy master sergeant with a southern accent and a talent for downing liters of beer without getting even a bit drunk, was the first to die.

Rando keeled over in the midst of clearing out a government housing complex. He came back in short order and bit two of the people he'd been sent there to try to save. They turned, attacked, and created others. It spread like a grass fire on a dry afternoon.

That was the morning of the third day. The last twenty-four hours had been a nightmare of sickness and attacks and running and hiding. Bolivar had spent two years in Iraq. There, he witnessed battles and attacks and bombings, but nothing compared to this. This was Hell on Earth.

He became separated from the other two remaining soldiers in his squad just before dawn when a pack of eight or so of the slow zombies shambled out of a shattered storefront window. Corporal Gwen Peduto and First Sergeant Clint Sawyer zigged while Bolivar zagged, and by the time he realized they'd gone in a different direction, more zombies were in the middle. Reconnecting was not an option. He pulled his pistol, shot at and missed a zombie. The gunshots drew a crowd of twenty more. As he ran, he stumbled over a dead body, and his pistol skittered down a sewage grate.

Bolivar sprinted into an alley where he found a rusted, green dumpster and climbed inside. His feet sunk into hot, rotting filth. The wet muck seeped into his boots and filled the crevices between his toes, but at least he felt safe, or as safe as possible under the circumstances.

As he settled into a sitting position on some trash, a gray rat the size of a small dog scurried out and ran across his legs. He went to knock it away, then realized it was the first live rat he'd seen since arriving in the city. The first living animal of any kind, actually. I won't hurt you, Mr. Rat. Just keep a healthy distance.

He cohabitated with the rat for at least two hours, looking out through one of the rust holes to the street beyond. He saw thousands of zombies in that time, but after a while, they slowed, and it reached a point where he had seen no one, living or dead, for the better part of forty minutes. The morning was already scorching, and the conditions in the dumpster were stifling. Sweat poured off his brow, and the aroma of hot trash nauseated him.

Bolivar eased the lid of the dumpster open. He grabbed hold of the metal and pulled himself up from the pile of garbage he'd settled into. His feet pulled loose from the grime with a wet smacking sound that, for some reason, reminded him of a late spring night when he was a horny, inexperienced teenager kissing Lisa Weiss in the back of his dad's hatchback. He swung his long legs over the edge of the dumpster and dropped to the pavement.

The dead-end alley was vacant, and he hugged the wall as he approached the street. To the right, a group of slow-moving zombies staggered up the road. To the left was emptiness, at least that's what he first thought. But then he spotted a wheelchair rocking forward and back, forward and back, a few inches at a time as its occupant tried to maneuver out of a jumble of bicycles, overturned trash cans, and the curb of the sidewalk.

Bolivar jogged toward the wheelchair and grabbed the handlebars. From the back, all he could see of the person was a mop of white hair.

"I've got you," he said as he pulled the chair from the debris as gently as possible.

Once it was clear of the rubble, he turned the chair around so he could face its fair-haired rider. What he saw was a dead man with his legs amputated at the knees. His head bobbed atop his neck. When his dead eyes caught Bolivar, they locked on him.

Bolivar stood motionless until the zombie dove out of the wheelchair and tumbled on top of him. It clawed at him with its ragged nails, and Bolivar stiff-armed it to hold it back. The zombie snapped its jaws, biting at the air. The stumps of its thighs kicked up and down in a swimming motion.

As Bolivar held the zombie up and away from him, yellow saliva seeped from its lips, and he had to turn his face sideways to keep the slimy drool from landing in his mouth. It hit his cheek instead and dribbled down his skin like warm honey.

He tried to hold the zombie off with one arm and reach for the knife he carried on his belt with the other, but the legless man was too heavy, and Bolivar could feel his grip slipping.

The zombie was top heavy and tilted downward, its face coming nearer and nearer to Bolivar's own. The sour smell of rot emanated from the creature's mouth, which was perilously close to his own.

Just as Bolivar's fingers wrapped around the shaft of his knife, the right side of the zombie's head blew out in a burst of brains and bone. He pushed the zombie away and looked to his left and saw Gwen Peduto running to him, her pistol still raised.

"That was a close one!" she said.

Bolivar climbed to his feet as she reached him. She was in her late twenties, over a decade younger than himself. Her brunette hair was pulled back in a bun that bulged from the bottom of her cap, and he noticed a fair amount of blood spattered on her uniform.

"I was pretty sure you bit it," she said and tittered. "Bad choice of words. Sorry."

Bolivar couldn't manage a laugh but offered a weak smile. "I thought the same for you. What about Sawyer?"

She glanced back in the direction from which she had come. Clay Sawyer hauled ass up the street, but a few dozen quick zombies weren't far behind. Sawyer was about the same age as Jorge. He was tall and wide with a shaved head and a bushy red beard that Jorge thought made him look like a lumberjack.

"Move! Move!" Sawyer screamed as he ran. He was still a hundred yards from them.

Peduto handed Bolivar a pistol. "Take this. It's only a nine, but there are six rounds left in the mag."

Bolivar chambered a round and flicked on the safety.

"I'd let the safety off if I were you."

Peduto was one of the soldiers that had requested he accompany them on the apartment building debacle, even though he should have been tending to casualties in the field hospital. Some of the younger soldiers thought it was good luck to have a medic along because they believed bad shit only happened when no one was around to fix it. He'd been happy to humor them, but that superstition had been disproved once and for all.

"What the fuck are you yahoo's waiting on?" Sawyer said. He was less than twenty-five yards away now. "Head due south!"

They did as told. Sawyer caught up to them, but the horde of zombies wasn't far behind.

"Where are we going?" Peduto asked.

"Wells Fargo. Orders came over the radio a couple minutes ago. All personnel are to report for immediate evac."

"And then what?" Bolivar asked.

"Operation Liberty Bell. At twelve hundred Juliet, they're firebombing the city. Everything from Roosevelt Cemetery to the airport."

At hearing that news, Bolivar slowed a step. "What about all the people? How do they get out?"

Sawyer didn't look back. "They don't. That's the point."

Peduto slowed to let Bolivar catch up to her. "Come on. Let's just get there first, then we'll figure it out."

The zombies were close enough to hear their throaty gasps and growls, and Bolivar picked up the pace.

CHAPTER NINE

IT HAD BEEN three days since Wim had burned his animals. His phone was out, as was the power, and he was cut off from the world. The cut off part didn't particularly bother him, but he found himself with what his mother would have called 'a bad case of the sulks' over the animals. That and doubts about what, if any, future remained for the farm.

The farm had been in his family for three generations, counting Wim. His grandfather on his mother's side was the first to break ground. He died when Wim was only four, and Wim didn't remember much about the man—couldn't even recall his actual first name for certain. The male influence in Wim's life had always been his Pa, and even though they butted heads here and there, his respect long outlasted his life.

The old man was a firm believer that if you worked hard enough and prayed long enough, anything was possible. When the farm failed after that bad summer when all the crops died, Pa could still work men one-third his age into the ground. He seemed capable of living forever, but less than two years later, he was the one in the ground. It wasn't sickness that put him there—at least not the physical kind—but in the end, it didn't matter. Dead was dead, regardless of the cause.

Wim was thirteen when Pa passed, and soon after, he informed his mother he was dropping out of school to take care of the farm. She gave him a little slap on the mouth, and that was the end of that.

So, the two of them, a teenage boy and his almost seventy-year-old mother, did the best they could to keep the family farm afloat. All things considered, they did an admirable job. The bills all got paid, and the animals were always well tended, too. They made enough money to survive, and that was all they needed.

Four years later, when Wim was a junior in high school, Mama's sugar got out of control, and she ended up in the hospital, where they first cut off her toe, then her foot, then the bottom part of her leg. When they said there was a wound that wouldn't heal on her other leg, she told them to pack their knives away for good. She never made it home.

Wim finished high school because he knew that's what Mama would have wanted, but he turned down offers from three different colleges. For the last seventeen years, he was never away from the farm, or his animals, for more than a few hours at a time.

In the absence of his parents, the pigs and chickens and cows had become his family. As much as he told himself they were all he needed, the loneliness wore on him. He'd go weeks at a time without talking to anyone but the livestock, and now they were dead too, and he was all alone.

The reminiscing wasn't getting him anywhere, though, and Wim decided three days was long enough to sulk.

———

THE BLAND GRAY SKY MIRRORED WIM'S MOOD. HE HADN'T BOTHERED TO collect his mail in days. So, when he made the long walk up the dirt lane that connected his farm to the county road and found the mailbox empty, he was more than a little perturbed. He slammed the mailbox closed and turned back to face the farm when a scraping sound drew his attention.

The noise came from around the blind tree-lined curve up the road, but Wim couldn't see anything. Whatever was making all the racket was getting closer, so Wim crossed his arms and decided to wait and see.

It was only a few moments until the source revealed itself. The blue uniform would have been a dead giveaway, but Wim didn't need it to know the person staggering down the road was Hoyt Mabrey, the man who had been delivering mail to the farm for close to thirty years.

Hoyt dragged the large mail sack behind him, and the canvas scraping against the rough pavement was the object causing so much noise. It was an odd sight, and Wim couldn't quite understand it.

"Hoyt? Where's your mail truck?"

Hoyt didn't respond. He just kept walking down the road.

"Are you all right?"

Hoyt turned his head toward Wim and staggered toward him. As he came closer, Wim saw that the man's skin had taken on a sickly gray pallor. His mouth hung open like a door with a broken hinge, and thick saliva, opaque with mucous, dribbled out.

When he was only a few yards away, Wim noticed the man's eyes were as dull and as gray as his skin, but they were still seeing. He looked at Wim, and a pained moan worked its way up his throat and fell out his mouth.

"Hoyt?"

The mailman was almost within arm's length now, and he reached out and swiped at Wim, who felt the displaced air rush by his face. Wim also caught a whiff of Hoyt's aroma. It was a scent that was common in the country: the smell of death.

"Oh, my God."

Wim took a step backward, then another. The zombie kept coming.

Wim turned and ran down the dirt road to the farm. He outpaced Hoyt, who progressed slowly but steadily, still dragging the mail sack behind him like an anchor.

When he reached the barn, Wim grabbed the double-barrel shotgun he'd earlier used to destroy the rats. He'd reloaded it after disposing of them and, at that time, wondered why he had even bothered. He flicked off the safety, then stood by the barn doors and watched the mailman trudge down the path.

Wim waited until Hoyt was about ten yards away and within range, then fired a round of buckshot into the zombie's chest.

The mailman staggered back a step as his blue uniform shirt disintegrated, and a gaping wound appeared beside the "Hoyt" name tag.

With little hesitation, Hoyt lurched forward again. It was like something out of a movie or a nightmare. Wim could see bits of shattered ribs through the tattered ribbons of flesh on the zombie's chest.

Wim had one more round left, and he allowed the mailman to get good and close. Hoyt was only a few feet away as Wim leveled off the barrel and aimed it at his head. Wim looked away as he squeezed the trigger but still caught the right side of the zombie's head shearing off in his peripheral vision.

A splash of dark, coagulated blood and light gray brains shot out of the gap where Hoyt's skull had gone missing. He toppled backward and landed on top of his mail sack.

Wim set the shotgun against the barn door and looked down at the dead mailman and wondered what to do next.

CHAPTER TEN

GRADY O'BAKER CHEWED his thin bottom lip as he stood outside his boss's closed office door. Ollie's voice had summoned him over the showroom intercom a few minutes earlier. As always when he heard his name boom over the loudspeakers, his stomach turned sour. He raised his hand to knock, lowered it, then made a second attempt.

Please, Father in Heaven, don't let this be anything bad. I'm trying so hard.

He gave a tepid rap just beside the nameplate declaring the space behind the door belonged to Oliver Benedict, CEO.

"It's open!" Ollie barked.

Grady eased the steel door open and leaned inside. "You wanted to see me, Mr. Benedict?"

Ollie glanced up from a mountain of manila folders and waved him in. He was barely into his thirties, but his ruddy red face carried the stress and blood pressure of someone twenty years older.

"Don't stand there like you got your thumb stuck up your goddamn ass."

Grady cringed at the blaspheme but tried not to show it as he stepped into the office. He started toward Ollie's desk, but Ollie pointed to the doorway. "Close the goddamn door!"

Grady did as told, then tiptoed across the room. He hesitated when he reached the chair. Ollie scowled, and Grady took a seat. They sat there in silence for a moment while Ollie sorted through the stack of folders. Grady, all five feet two inches of him, felt like a boy waiting to be scolded by the principal.

Please give me strength, Father. I can withstand all adversity with your guidance.

Eventually, Ollie extracted a folder from the pile and waved it in Grady's pale, worried face.

"You know what this is?" Ollie asked and didn't wait for an answer. "Your personnel folder."

Grady thought it was quite thick, considering he'd only been working at Benedict Electronics for four months.

Ollie pulled out a fistful of yellow slips. "And these are customer complaints against you."

Grady sucked in a mouthful of stale office air, and the sour sickness in his belly turned into a molten lake of pain as one or more of his ulcers sent up a geyser of acid. "I'm sorry, Mr. Benedict. I always try to do my best and treat the customers in a Godly manner."

Ollie flipped through the complaints. "That's the problem. 'Salesman kept talking about God.' 'Asked where we went to church.' 'Asked us if we wanted to pray with him.' 'Invited us to his church.'" He looked at Grady with visible disgust.

To Grady, these seemed the exact opposite of complaints. "I don't understand, sir."

"With you, it's always this holy roller Jesus Christ Almighty bullshit. People don't want to be preached to. They just want to buy a goddamn TV, and your job is to sell it to them. Nothing more."

Why is he saying this? It's like the world's gone upside down.

"But I... That's my nature."

"You're fired, Grady."

He thought he must have heard wrong. Fired? For being kind? For trying to share God's love? "Sir? There must be a mistake."

"Turn in your uniform shirts by the end of the week, or they'll be deducted from your final pay." Ollie closed Grady's folder and added it to a new, smaller pile. "It's a goddamn shame you couldn't fit in here. All you had to do was keep your mouth shut."

Grady stared into Ollie's tired, hazel eyes so long and intense that the big man looked away. "The Devil has hold of you, sir," Grady said. "Avarice has turned your soul black and rotten, but no one is beyond salvation. And I forgive you."

"Fuck off." Ollie took another folder, and that was Grady's cue to go. As he fled the office, his former boss sneezed twice in rapid succession.

Grady turned around and said, without the slightest hint of sarcasm, "God bless you."

———

THE DAYCARE SMELLED LIKE POOP, AND GRADY SAID A SILENT PRAYER THAT the source was not his son. When Tara Charles, the iron-haired owner of Tender Tots, stepped into the room and met him with a scowl on her face, he suspected the worst. When he then saw that Josiah, his ten-year-old boy, was wearing lime green sweatpants two sizes too big rather than the khaki trousers he'd begun the day in, those suspicions were confirmed.

A dozen or so children, most under the age of five, played with a variety of toys, games, and each other. Only Josiah sat alone. He faced the corner of the playroom and was stacking wooden blocks with big, primary colored letters. His wood tower spelled out SVAEKC.

"I wasn't expecting you until six," Tara said.

Grady had rehearsed what to say about that during his half-hour bus ride. "I was laid off today," was the most diplomatic and least emasculating response he'd been able to summon.

Tara's icy stare thawed slightly. "I'm sorry to hear that. The job market is... challenging, right now."

Grady knew this all too well. Before being hired to sell appliances and electronics, he'd been unemployed for fourteen months. "Yes, it is. But God will provide. He always does."

Tara snorted, and the look on her face revealed that a sarcastic comment was about to come, but Grady looked past her to his son. A long, yellow string of snot hung from the boy's right nostril. Tara followed Grady's gaze.

"Joe had an accident no more than an hour ago. His pants are still in the laundry. You can wait if you like."

It annoyed Grady that she called him Joe. He'd asked her several times not to, and he sometimes wondered if she did it to irritate him. "No, I'll get them another time."

She nodded. "I'd appreciate it if you could bring more diapers. Good ones from here on. Those generic ones aren't adequate at all."

"I will. I'm sorry." He chewed his lip before continuing, "But I must take Josiah out of daycare. Until I find a new job."

Tara's frost returned. "He'll have to go back on the waiting list."

"I understand. God willing, the wait won't be long."

"And you'll be billed for this entire week per your contract."

"Yes, Ma'am. Charge it to my card."

Tara turned away and moved to a group of toddlers, never even casting a glance toward Josiah. Grady crossed to his son and drummed his fingers on the top of Josiah's thin, blond hair, which was a perfect match for Grady's own. The boy's attention didn't leave the blocks, not even when Grady wiped the snot streamer from his face.

"Hey now, Josiah. It's time to go home."

Josiah ignored or didn't hear him—Grady was never sure which—and stacked another block. Q.

Grady had to reach under his armpits and lift him off the floor. The sweatpants threatened to fall, but the bulky diaper the boy wore, which Grady noticed was adorned with pink cartoon unicorns, gave enough resistance to hold them up.

Grady led his son toward the exit and opened the door. Tara didn't respond as they left, and Grady said a silent prayer that God would teach her compassion. She certainly lacked it at the present.

———

HOME WAS A THREE-ROOM APARTMENT OF APPROXIMATELY TWO hundred square feet. Josiah's toys—puzzles mostly, the boy had a real talent for them—cluttered the living room-slash-kitchenette. Grady and Josiah shared the lone bedroom.

Altogether, it was about the size of a cheap motel room, and it cost Grady almost eight hundred dollars a month. He didn't know how they'd be able to afford even that much if he didn't get another job in short order, but God always provided.

They'd had a real home once, in a time Grady wistfully thought of as "before." In that home, there'd been a wife and a mother. Her name was Ruth, which she always said was a plain name for a plain Jane, but to Grady, she was anything but plain.

She'd been the girl of his dreams when he met her at church camp when he was seventeen, and she was fifteen. It took until the next summer before he could convince her to give him a chance, but once she agreed, Grady never looked back.

They married the summer after Ruth graduated high school, and, for a few years, everything was as close to perfect as he could have imagined. Yes, the baby they both longed for wasn't quick to come, but all in due time. God had a plan.

Six years and no babies later, Ruth had fallen into a deep abyss. They tried fertility treatments and medicines, but nothing seemed to matter. When Grady insisted they keep praying, Ruth admitted that she had lost faith. Her words shook Grady, but he rebounded. After that, he prayed not only for a child, but for God to come back into Ruth's life.

On one of the darkest nights, when Ruth was away with friends, leaving Grady all alone and everything was silent, he begged God to hear him. For God to answer his prayers. And God did answer.

Grady never told anyone this—he knew what they'd say—but he was certain the voice inside his head was that of God our Father as sure as he knew his own name and date of birth. God promised Grady that His plan was going as needed, that all would be well, and that, in time, Grady would understand. The comfort Grady received from that voice was all he needed to get him through, even when Ruth grew cold and distant.

Three years after that, God graced them with Josiah. He was a perfect eight pounds, two-ounce baby boy, and Grady swore he came out of the womb smiling. His cherubic grin lifted Ruth out of her depression, and their family was whole.

When Josiah was two years old and still hadn't spoken, not even mama or dada, or taken to potty training, Ruth insisted they take him to a specialist. Grady thought it an overreaction, but after countless appointments with experts, tests, and scans, Josiah was diagnosed as autistic.

The following three years were hard—even Grady would have admitted that. As time passed, he accepted that Josiah wasn't going to get better. Ruth took it worse.

One day, Grady came home to find Josiah locked in his room and Ruth nowhere to be found. He filed a missing person's report, and, for almost four months, he devoted every moment of his life to finding his missing wife. He gave interviews to reporters, appeared on local television, and even paid for five huge billboards and a 1-800 number people could call with tips. No calls came, but a letter did. It was short but got the point across.

"I'm not missing. Stop looking for me. I'm not coming back. Everything is yours."

Even though she hadn't bothered to sign it, Grady knew his wife's handwriting. He told the police, and the search was called off, and that was the end of it. His sole income as a church bookkeeper was far from enough to pay the mortgage, and they lost their nice home in the suburbs. That's how they ended up in a rundown row house apartment in Baltimore.

Ruth wasn't all that had left him. God, too, had gone silent. It had been almost five years since Grady had heard that warm, loving voice telling him it was all going to be okay, and he longed for its return.

Grady fried a pan of hamburger helper while Josiah stared blankly at Mister Rogers on the TV. He stirred in the fake cheese sauce and thought he heard a gunshot outside as Fred sang about it being a beautiful day in the neighborhood. No, it's not, Grady thought. We haven't had a beautiful day for a long, long time.

At the other side of the apartment, Josiah broke out in a fit of wet, thick coughs, which lasted a full half a minute. Grady looked above his son where a painting of Jesus in the garden at Gethsemane hung on the wall.

I beg of you, God, please embrace us and watch over us. We need you now, maybe more than ever. Please make our lives better.

His faith was so strong that he actually believed God would.

CHAPTER ELEVEN

THE HARD VINYL made a gross farting noise as Mina Costell shifted side to side in her chair and tried to get comfortable. Hospitals were already such horrible places with the beeping machines, the overwhelming smell of antiseptic, the barely controlled chaos, and, of course, the sickness. You'd think the least they could do is provide comfortable and quiet seating.

She folded and unfolded her hands, smoothed the wrinkles in her skirt, and, with nothing else to distract herself, looked at the bed beside her where her father tossed and turned. His labored breaths were thick and full of phlegm. Every once in a while, his breathing would stop altogether, and, each time, Mina held hers.

As she stared at his leathery face, its left side pulled down into an obscene grimace. Mina wished, no, she prayed, that the old bastard would just die already.

Instead, he woke up.

Vernon Costell looked around the room with confused eyes, and for a fleeting moment, Mina pitied him. But when he saw his daughter, anger replaced the confusion, and his beady, black eyes zeroed in on her like missiles. "What am I doing in the goddamn hospital?"

Mina melted into the chair and looked at her hands in her lap rather than her father. "You went unconscious, Daddy. I couldn't wake you up."

Vernon squirmed into a sitting position and, in doing so, caused the nasal cannula feeding oxygen into his nose to pull askew and yank his nostrils upward like a pig snout. "You know I don't want nothing to do with hospitals, you little bitch. Don't you got any brains left in that thick skull of yours, Birdie?"

The instant he used that name, Mina was twelve years old again. That was the first time he had called her Birdie. She was standing in the hot, cramped kitchen of their section eight apartment, her wiry hair pulled back in pigtails, and she wore the bright yellow dress she bought all on her own. It didn't matter that it came from the thrift store or that it only cost a quarter. She picked it out, and, for the very first time in her life, she felt pretty.

"Do you like my new dress, Daddy?" she'd asked him.

Vernon glanced up at her as he gobbled up his food like he was afraid someone would beat him to it. "Look like one of those birdies to me. Ones that peck the nigger seed off the flowers in the fall."

Layla, her younger sister by less than a year, burst out laughing, spraying a mouthful of mashed potatoes in the process. That made Vernon cackle. He pointed at Mina. "Don't she look like a birdie? Skinny little legs? Big beaky nose?"

Layla flapped her arms. "Mina's a birdie! Tweet, tweet!"

Seeking an ally, Mina turned to her mother, who washed dishes by hand at the sink. But her mother kept her head down and her mouth shut. Something Mina learned to do all too well in time.

Even though Mina never wore the yellow dress again, Vernon called her Birdie often after that day, especially when he wanted to hurt her. Through the years, he hurt her a lot. Sometimes with his hands, like when he slapped her so hard that his wedding band broke her front tooth in half. Sometimes with his feet, like the time she missed her curfew by six minutes, and he told her she was a cock-sucking whore who needed to mind her place. That night, he shoved her onto the floor, then kicked her over and over again with his heavy work boot clad feet until she managed to crawl under the kitchen table. She passed blood for almost a week after. But, for a girl with a name as beautiful as Wilhelmina, all the beatings put together didn't cause her as much pain as being called Birdie.

Layla got pregnant when she was thirteen, knocked up by the maintenance man who spent too much time making repairs in their apartment. He married her, but they both died in a car wreck before the baby could even be born. A couple years later, their mother died of a brain bleed supposedly caused by falling down the steps but more likely caused by Vernon's fists. Mina envied both of them because they got out.

When Vernon was forty-nine and digging out a drainage ditch for the city, he suffered a major stroke. His left side was useless, but he still had his right to keep her in line. His disability insurance barely made ends meet, so Mina, who was then seventeen and had dreams of being a nurse or a teacher, got hired on as a chambermaid for a local hotel and spent the best years of her life cleaning up other people's messes.

If anything, the stroke made her daddy meaner. It was easier to slip out of the way of his fists, but he had other ways of punishing her. His favorite trick was soiling his pants on purpose, even though he was perfectly capable of using the walker and going to the bathroom on his own.

"Birdie! Get in here and clean my ass!" he'd holler.

The first time Mina had to wash the putrid shit out of his crack and off his shriveled balls, she threw up. Vernon heard her retching and cackled like a hyena. That wasn't the last time he'd made her puke, but it was the last time she let him hear her.

All told, it had been thirty-nine years of cruelty, and, on more days than not, Mina just hoped that one of them would wake up dead. She didn't even care much which one. She just wanted it to end.

Vernon reached over with his hand and slapped her thigh hard.

"Quit your wool gatherin' and fix this fucking tube--"

Mina glanced at him and saw his piggish nostrils flared and his eyes wide. His entire body tensed and then went into a violent spasm that seemed like it would never end. But it did, and he collapsed backward. It took her a moment to react; she just stared into his eyes. When his pupils dilated, she snapped out of her daze. She rushed to the door and leaned into the hospital hallway. "I think my daddy just died!"

CHAPTER TWELVE

BUNDY OWNED what he considered to be an admirable collection of firearms. From rare long guns like an 1892 Winchester Saddle Ring Carbine 25-20 Caliber Rifle and a Springfield Model 1842 Percussion Musket to small arms such as a U.S. Simeon North Flintlock Pistol Model 1816 and a Colt Model 1860 Army Revolver.

He'd fired all of them at least once. Guns were more than his hobby. Guns were his way of life. So when a friend of a friend of a shooting buddy offered him a chance to buy a genuine, fully automatic Hellpup AK-47, he wasn't about to let the opportunity pass him by. The fact that buying said gun was illegal didn't bother him that much. Bundy had no plans to rob a bank or shoot up a school. He wanted to own it just because.

He met with Jim, the seller, outside what Jim said was his favorite bar, a street-side dive named Mel's, which promised Good Eats, Good Company, and Unlimited Wings every Friday. Bundy liked wings and thought he might take them up on the offer after their transaction was complete.

Jim was an intense, bearded fellow who looked like he'd seen some time in combat. Bundy handed him five hundred dollars in twenties, but Jim didn't hand him the Hellpup. Instead, he arrested him. Bundy never even got to touch the gun. Or try the wings.

His real name was Rudolph Polakowski, but ever since Hulk Hogan had squared off against King Kong Bundy in Wrestlemania 2, everyone called him Bundy. And that was fine. It certainly beat Lardass or Wide Load or Porkbeast or any of the other taunts that had been hurled his way since the first grade.

He was a large boy who grew into a mountain of a man. Bundy stood six feet seven inches tall. He was far too large for regular scales. Once, he thought it would be amusing to step onto one of the truck weighing stations they had out front of the scrap yard. He was about four hundred and forty pounds then, but that was thirty years ago when he was still growing. He now considered his weight to be inde-terminate. After the arrest and conviction, Rudolph Polakowski became Inmate 2089349. He still preferred Bundy.

He'd been a guest at SCI Pittsburgh for about two months when the prison physician discovered the lump on his testicle during an other-wise routine physical. Bundy had wondered why the nervous little man was spending so much time fondling his junk, but after the doc finally told him to pull up his pants, he broke the news.

Bundy wasn't too worried. After all, he had two balls, so losing one wasn't anything to lose sleep over. Normally, a van would have taken Bundy and the other seven prisoners needing medical care to the hospital, but due to his extra-extra-extra-large frame, a bus was procured instead.

Around noon, they traded their cells for the police blue prison bus. Just in case anyone might confuse it with a school or public transit bus, "Department of Corrections" was stenciled on the front, back, and both sides in bold white lettering.

The day was already hot, and the heat bounced off the pavement in shimmery, rainbow-colored waves. Bundy was sweating through his orange prison jumpsuit before he even stepped onto the bus. His uniform was the biggest size they made, but the zippered front still threatened to burst.

He and the other inmates were handcuffed, and the cuffs were attached to belly chains. Bundy required two chains to be locked together to fit around his waist. The restraints gave his hands about five inches of movement in any given direction.

Bundy only recognized one of the other inmates, a beanpole everyone called Cob because he didn't just eat the corn but chewed on the cob until it disappeared. Probably why he's going to the hospital, Bundy thought. That can't be healthy.

The rest of the group was hacking like they had a whooping cough. It seemed like almost everyone in the prison was sick. According to the lifers, that was normal. "One gets sick; we all get sick," they said. But these six were particularly ill.

Two guards chaperoned the inmates. Errickson, the younger of the two, suffered from little man syndrome with bodybuilder arms and no visible fat. He sported a high and tight, nerd glasses, and a bad attitude. He stood beside the bus door and was all too eager to herd them on. "Squeeze your fat ass in there, Bundy," Errickson ordered. "If it'll fit through the door, that is."

Bundy ambled along in no particular hurry. "I'm coming, Boss. Don't work yourself up."

Errickson scowled and rested his hand on his utility belt, which contained his collapsible baton, taser, and pepper spray. Bundy held his handcuffed hands up before him to mime surrender. "Don't taze me, bro."

Bundy chuckled. Errickson didn't.

The bus sagged down when Bundy stepped aboard, and the old metal creaked as he climbed the two steps and moved toward the seats. The other guard, Allebach, was pushing fifty and much more relaxed than his young partner.

"You good?" Allebach asked as Bundy moved sideways through the narrow aisle.

"Sure thing, Boss."

Bundy was the last prisoner on. The rest sat side by side, cuffed together in pairs. Bundy got his own seat. Being huge had its advantages.

Allebach took a seat at the back of the bus while Errickson stood watch at the front. The driver, a wheezy old fart who looked like he should have retired a decade ago, looked over his shoulder at his passengers. "That everyone?"

Errickson nodded. "Hit the road, Pop."

Bundy couldn't see the driver, but he suspected the man sneered. He certainly would have.

CHAPTER THIRTEEN

JULI VILLAREAL CHAIN-SMOKED Camels as she sat in front of the gigantic LCD screen and watched Donald in the Kitchen on the Home Shopping Channel. She didn't care if Donald was going gray, getting soft around the middle and queerer than Elton John. On days like today, he was her whole world.

"And if six inches isn't enough, we also have an eight for those of you who appreciate a few extra inches," Donald said with a smile and a wink. "And don't even get me started on the ten inch! Oh, lordy!"

Juli laughed out loud. LOLed, as she thought her kids would say, only they wouldn't actually say that, of course. Oh, that Donald was so naughty sometimes. She grabbed the phone and punched in the HSC number without even looking. It rang twice.

"Thank you for calling the Home Shopping Channel. How may we brighten your day?"

"I was calling about the Venice Cookware Donald's selling."

"Oh, yes, Ma'am. Would you like to place an order?"

"Actually, I already own a set. I thought maybe I could give a testimonial on the air."

Juli had given two live testimonials in the past, and both times, she got so excited that she thought she might pee her pants. Donald had talked to her on the air and thanked her for her call. It was heavenly.

"I'm sorry, Ma'am, but we already have two other callers waiting to share their experiences with the product. Are you sure you don't need another set? These just became available in McIntosh red."

Juli's eyes widened. Her pans were boring silver. McIntosh red? That was too good to pass up.

"Yes, I would!"

She rattled off her name, and the salesman pulled up her account. Juli Villareal was a superb customer at HSC, and they had all her info on file.

She hadn't always been a shopaholic. From ages twenty-two to thirty-six, she was a blissfully happy stay-at-home mother and a darned good one. Everyone said so.

Her twins, Matt and Marcy, were everything she could have ever wanted. And her husband, Mark, was the type of man every girl grew up wanting to marry. He was handsome and kind and a good provider. He'd been the top salesman at Evergreen Insurance for twelve years running. It was the perfect upper-middle-class life. Until it wasn't.

Four years ago, she was trying to find a video of Marcy's dance solo on Mark's iPhone when she uncovered a clip of a young blonde woman with enormous breasts treating a penis like it was a lollipop. There was a perfect, round mole at the base of the penis. A mole that was much too familiar for Juli to mistake.

When Juli confronted him with the video, Mark admitted the affair. The blonde with the big boobs was his colleague. He promised to end it, and Juli believed he had. He even transferred to another office to ease Juli's mind.

It helped to some extent, but their marriage was like a piece of china that someone had dropped and glued back together. It seemed fine from a distance, but if examined up close, you could see the cracks that would never go away.

Juli kept herself busy being the best mother she could be. She never missed a soccer match, dance recital, awards ceremony, or little league game. She chaperoned school trips and volunteered for the PTA. She took the twins to the mall and the movies and amusement parks.

They were best friends—the three musketeers. Until they weren't.

About the time the twins started their journey through puberty, their desire to hang out with their mother faded like a bright cloth left out too long in the sun. Marcy broke off first.

She needed a new dress for the Christmas Pageant, and Juli was excited to take her shopping, but Marcy said she'd rather have her friends go with her to pick it out. It was a throwaway remark, and the girl didn't mean to hurt her mother's feelings, but to Juli, it was like someone had chopped off her left arm.

About a year later, she surprised Matt with tickets to see the new Transformers movie in Imax on opening night. She'd bought them weeks in advance and wasn't even sure what Imax was, but it sounded exciting. Only when she handed the tickets to Matt, he said he was too old to go to the movies with his mom. He must have seen the pain wash over her and quickly said they could still go *this* time, but the damage was done.

Her family didn't need her anymore, but at least she had Donald in the Kitchen. Her brand new set of McIntosh red cookware only cost her $139.99, and they even split it into four easy payments. Life wasn't so bad after all.

The front door banged open. Matt walked in, talking into his cell phone, "I can't tonight. I have practice at six."

Juli looked toward him, hoping for a 'Hi, Mom,' but didn't even garner a nod.

"Yeah. Okay. Yeah, we'll go this weekend. I promise. Uh huh. Love you, too." He tossed down his book bag beside the door and kicked off his Nikes.

"Hello, Matt."

He glanced at his mother. "Oh. Hi."

The boy was tall like his father and even more handsome. His blue eyes stood out against his olive skin and patches of black stubble grew on his cleft chin, making him look more like a twenty-year-old than his true age of fifteen.

"Was that Laura?"

His brow furrowed. "No. Elise. I broke up with Laura a month ago. Jesus!"

"Sorry. Sorry. Don't bite my head off."

He looked to the kitchen. "What's for dinner?"

Despite a kitchen filled with high-quality cookware and gadgets, Juli hadn't given it much thought. She considered the options. "There's some lasagna in the freezer. I'll heat it up."

"We had lasagna last week!"

"That's why they're called leftovers, my son. They won't kill you."

"Whatever."

He sneezed twice without covering his mouth, spraying spittle over the granite countertops.

"Bless you."

Matt stomped up the stairs to his room, and Juli heard the door slam shut. She climbed off the couch, grabbed a paper towel and wiped off the counter.

I wonder if he's got that bug that Marcy has, she thought. Marcy had woken up that morning coughing and sneezing almost nonstop. Juli had offered to take her to the doctor, but Marcy had only glared, took a Sudafed, and said, 'I'm fine!' before fleeing the house like she was making a jailbreak.

There was so much love in the Villareal household Juli almost couldn't bear it.

CHAPTER FOURTEEN

IT WAS a quarter of one in the afternoon, and the boy who cut Emory Prescott's lawn should have been there by noon. Emory paced back and forth on the porch, casting frequent, furtive glances toward the long, bricked driveway. He kept expecting to discover him but kept ending up disappointed.

Christopher, the boy, was ordinarily quite timely and had not been late once in the two summers he'd been under Emory's employ. The old man was getting anxious.

He wasn't worried about the lawn. Spring had been dry, and the grass had grown less than an inch from the week prior. Emory was upset because he'd become fond of the boy and his visits. Sometimes, he didn't even bother Christopher to take the mower out of the garage. They would simply sit on the big porch and sip sun tea and chat.

It was an odd pair; that was for certain. Emory was seventy-eight years old, but his trim build and good health made him appear at least a decade younger. Christopher was more than sixty years his junior. He wore his pants so low that his boxer shorts showed, and Emory took more than a little enjoyment watching his nebby neighbors stare as the boy strutted about.

Emory had always hated Fox Chapel, with all its bankers and lawyers and local pseudo celebrities. He had only moved there at the demand of Grant, his partner of almost thirty years, who pleaded that he wanted to live in a "good section of the city" after growing up poor and scared in the Hill District. Emory obliged but always resented him for it.

Grant was twelve years his junior. When they met, he was a dance major at the city's premier art school. Emory saw him for the first time when he was at the school to give away some of his family's money. As the superintendent gushed over his generous donation, Emory's attention wandered, and he caught sight of the nineteen-year-old beauty as he twirled and floated across the stage during rehearsal.

Emory stayed until the class ended and waited for Grant to exit the changing room. When he did, he saw the young man was stunning up close, too. He asked Grant if he'd ever been to New York City, and when he said no, Emory offered to take him. Within a year, they were living together and would have married if such a thing were possible.

The first few years of their coupling were full of love and passion, but as that wore off, the differences in their personalities took a toll. Grant loved the money. Emory did, too, mainly for the freedom it provided, but Grant became addicted to it. Shopping trips to London and Paris. Vacations in Tahiti and Tuscany. The winter home he had to have in Key West.

Emory loved making his beautiful beau happy, but sometimes, happiness seemed as elusive to Grant as a trip to Jupiter. He acted the part, went to all the galas, sat on numerous charity boards, and dined with the city's elite—the things rich people do—but Emory often thought his lover never looked as happy as he had that first time he saw him, jumping into the air under the purple and pink stage lights.

As they grew older, it was clear their love story wasn't the storybook romance Emory always longed for. Neither broached the subject of separating, and, as far as Emory knew, there were no trysts or affairs, but they felt more like roommates living under one huge roof. Ships meeting only occasionally at port. Emory sometimes felt his greatest failure in life was that he could never give his one true love the happiness he deserved.

Their glorious mansion on the hill felt more like a prison than a home for the past fourteen months. That was after a three-pack-a-day smoking habit and lung cancer put Grant in the ground and "ever after" became "never was."

Emory kept meaning to find a realtor and list the house. He wanted rid of it and fancied he might buy one of those obnoxious motor coaches with names like Born Free or Renegade and drive it around the country while there was still a country worth seeing. Maybe it would even inspire him to write the book he'd always talked about writing, and which Grant had so encouraged, but never got around to doing.

Just as he began to think he must have mixed up his days—something that happened more often than he cared to think about lately—the whiny drone of Christopher's moped came within earshot. A grin that deepened the road map of wrinkles that etched Emory's face appeared, and he skipped down the porch steps to meet the boy in the driveway.

Christopher's moped skidded to a stop, and he jumped off without bothering to drop the kickstand. It crashed onto its side as the boy yanked off his helmet. He was tall and built like an athlete, which he was. Emory had gone to every one of his football games and cheered him on like he was his own son.

The boy's actual father had never been around, and his mother had died in a traffic accident a few years earlier. He lived with an aunt who worked too much just to stay ahead of the bill collectors, and

Emory knew much of the money he paid Christopher also went toward those bills.

Emory had given him generous Christmas bonuses and raises at every opportunity but was wary of appearing as if he was trying to buy the boy's affection. He was enamored with Christopher and didn't want it to show. Nothing sexual—Emory's sail hadn't flown past half mast in over a decade, and that didn't bother him in the least—but the boy's very presence was intoxicating.

Emory lusted after Christopher's youth because, even if he was less than two full calendars away from becoming an octogenarian, he still felt like he was Christopher's age in his mind. He would have eagerly traded everything he owned for that youth, for the chance to live life all over again. Impossible, of course, but the daydreams alone could brighten his mood on even the darkest day.

"I was worried you weren't—" Emory stopped when he saw Christopher's panicked, wide-eyed expression. "What's the matter?"

"It's my aunt. I think she's dying."

"Oh, my. I'm so sorry, Christopher. You certainly didn't have to come here today if she--"

"I need you to help her. You have to. Right now!"

"I—" Emory paused, confused. "Why didn't you call for an ambulance?"

The boy pulled his cell phone from his pocket. "The phones are all out. Nine-one-one doesn't answer. I tried the hospital, too, but it won't go through, either."

Emory tried his own cell, a Nokia so old it was practically an antique. He attempted to make a call and in his ear heard only the dull, continuous tone signaling a line out of order.

"Please, Mr. Prescott, I didn't know where else to go."

The boy, all six feet and sixteen years of him, was on the verge of tears.

"Of course. Of course, I'll help, Christopher. Get in the Mercedes."

CHAPTER FIFTEEN

EIGHT MONTHS IN CULINARY SCHOOL, and this was the result. Slicing off fatty roast beef and gristly ham and shoving it onto plates at the Hearty Buffet.

Mead hadn't graduated from the culinary academy, of course. He rarely finished anything. He dropped out of high school junior year. He had a nine-month marriage when he was twenty-three. He had a kid that he hadn't seen in three years. No "Father of the Year" or "World's Greatest Dad" t-shirts coming in his future, that was for sure.

Being a chef would be different, though. He'd wanted to be a chef since he was seven years old and always knew it was his destiny. But culinary school wasn't any different than high school. Asshole know-it-all-teachers that treated him like shit. Uppity classmates who refused to talk to him after realizing he was white trash. He wanted to cook, but he couldn't deal with that bullshit. Life was too short.

He was twenty-nine and thought he'd have accomplished something meaningful by now, but he hadn't. This job would turn things around, though.

It was close to his shitty apartment, which was good because his rusted-out Cavalier knocked like the engine would blow any day now. The nine dollars an hour pay wasn't great, but it wasn't terrible for the area. And best of all, he'd finally get to do something he loved.

That's what he thought when he landed the job. Reality was less romantic. The most cooking he'd done in three months was frying omeletes every Sunday morning, but even those eggs came pre-scrambled and poured out of a box.

Every disgusting piece of food on the buffet, except the salad, came in frozen. Occasionally, they'd fire up an oven, but most of it got nuked in the industrial microwaves they kept out of sight in the back. Yet, the poor, fat clientele that voted the buffet "Johnstown's Best Value Eatery" three years running ate the shit up like it was farm fresh and made of gold.

A wheezy, old woman with blue hair sidled up beside Mead's station and looked at the two hunks of grayish meat. "Is there MSG in this?" she asked.

"Probably."

"I can't eat MSG. Gives me the trots." She rubbed her ample belly as she said that.

"That's why we have plenty of bathrooms, Ma'am."

She examined him for a moment, trying to decide whether he was being rude or funny, decided on the latter, then chuckled.

"Give me a slice of each. You only live once. Isn't that what you kids say?"

It flattered Mead to be referred to as a kid, even if she was old enough to be his grandmother, and gave her two extra large portions. She grinned at her haul, but before she could walk off, she was surprised by an almost violent sneeze. Ropes of green snot hit the plexiglass covering the meat with a wet *thwack*. Mead was never so happy for the sneeze guard in his life.

"Scuse me," she said and didn't bother cleaning up her expelled fluids before walking away.

Mead tried to ignore the ooze, but, as it precariously neared the edge and risked dripping onto the ham, he gave up, pulled a food-stained rag from his apron and wiped it away. A foggy haze remained behind, but he pretended not to see it as he deposited the rag straight into the trash bin.

He noticed that there was a lot of sneezing going on around him. Coughing, too. The Hearty Buffet was hardly the pinnacle of health, but the amount of audible sickness unnerved him. Wasn't cold and flu season supposed to be in the fall?

A middle-aged man topped with a ten-gallon cowboy hat on a twelve-gallon head was next in line. He was about as wide as he was tall and his plate was already overflowing with food. "I'll take the beef. Slice her thick."

Mead did as told, and, after he moved one slice to the plate, the cowboy tipped his head. "One more."

"Sure thing, Partner."

Cowboy's grin faded, and he stomped away after getting his second helping.

A six-year-old that Mead could tell was a brat just by looking at his carrot red hair and pointed, squirrelly face sprinted toward his station, almost crashing into it. He stared up at Mead quizzically. "You look funny."

So do you, twerp, Mead thought but didn't say. He was aware that he looked different. The hairnet containing his thick, drab brown locks bulged out at the sides like Princess Leia's buns. Add in a pencil-thin mustache and a head shaped like a Lego character, and he got his share of curious looks.

Before Mead could put on his fake smile and ask the brat what he wanted, a scream drew everyone's attention.

"My Henry!"

The voice was shrill and old. Mead looked for the source and saw it was Blue Hair. In the booth across from her, a man, presumably the aforementioned Henry, had slumped face first into his instant mashed potatoes.

Even though Mead had only been there a few months, this was not the first person he'd seen die at the buffet. If Henry was indeed dearly departed, he'd be the third fatality on Mead's shifts alone. Says a lot about our clientele.

Cindy, a chestnut-haired waitress who put both the big and beautiful in BBW, and an Asian busboy named Pan, rushed to Henry's side. Pan pulled Henry's face free from the potatoes. White starch and brown gravy filled in his wrinkles like spackle. Pan held his ear close to Henry's mouth.

"Call an ambulance!" Cindy shouted, and Mead couldn't help but notice her tits jiggled like jello as she yelled.

Pan's face shriveled up as he tried to listen for breathing sounds over the growing commotion around him. Then, his squinted eyes grew wide, and he shoved Henry backward in the booth.

Mead saw a spurt of red and noticed that Pan's ear, or at least the bottom half of it anyway, was missing. Pan clasped his hand over his ear and screamed something in Chinese or Korean; Meade wasn't sure which. Maybe even Thai, for all he knew.

Cindy grabbed on to Pan, pressing her ample bosom against him, and tried to lead him away, but by that point, pretty much everyone in the restaurant had crowded around to gawk at what had happened.

Everyone but Mead, who was content to take in the events from afar. While all the lookie loos focused on Pan with his one and a half ears, Mead watched Henry. What he saw was the elderly man slumped back into the booth and chewing on the hard cartilage of Pan's ear like it was a piece of saltwater taffy.

"Henry! What are you doing?" his blue-haired wife shrieked. She reached across the table and toward Henry's mouth where a piece of Pan's ear extruded and tried to pull it free.

"Bad idea, lady," Mead muttered to himself.

Bad idea, indeed. Henry snarled like a dog and snapped at her. He caught the first knuckles of her middle and index fingers between his yellow choppers and bit them clean off.

She screamed again, but that faded away when she fainted and sprawled across the table.

Someone else shrieked, and Mead found himself longing for a return to the coughs and sneezes. This time, he saw Cindy with the huge, jiggly titties he so longed to bury his face in, squealing in agony as Pan took a massive bite out of the side of her neck.

Everything shifted into fast-forward after that. Mead saw Blue Hair rise from her faint, grab the arm of a teen with one of those out-of-fashion Justin Bieber haircuts and devour it.

Cindy pounced on a woman in a motorized scooter. Pan moved on to a waiter. Then the Bieber wannabe had his teeth buried in the plus-sized stomach of the cowboy. It seemed like everyone at the buffet was eating someone or being eaten.

It spread at lightning speed, one after another after another. And through it all, Mead watched Henry casually gnaw away at his wife's fingertips.

His attention was diverted when he caught the little ginger who had earlier almost taken out the meat station staring at him. The brat's left eye hung from its socket and dangled back and forth like a yoyo at the end of its string. He had a gaping wound in his neck that gushed blood by the pint, turning his lower body crimson.

The brat sprinted toward his station for the second time, only this time Mead wasn't afraid he'd upset the cart. He feared for his life. Mead shoved the wheeled cart toward him, knocking the boy onto his back.

The cart tipped over and fell onto the brat, but he squirmed out from beneath it with little effort. Then he jumped on top of it and leaped into the air, diving straight for Mead.

The kid hit him in the chest and wrapped his skinny legs around Mead's waist to hold on. He clawed and scratched at Mead, who desperately held him back. The brat's jaws snapped together so hard Mead thought his teeth would break.

With his free hand, Mead grabbed the large serving fork. He looked into the brat's eyes, or eye, as it was. The pupil was fully dilated, and he couldn't see but a hint of the iris. It looked dead, like a shark's eyes.

The little fucker's a zombie.

Mead plunged the two prongs of the fork into the brat's good eye. He felt it pop like a water balloon, and bloody, vitreous gel splashed out. He kept pushing the fork into the cavity until he buried it up to the handle. It was only then he noticed the brat had ceased moving.

Mead shoved him away, and the lifeless body hit the carpeted floor with a muffled thud.

"Take that, you little ginger zombie fuck!"

Mead looked up and saw everyone in the restaurant staring back at him.

They ran all at once. Mead spun on his heels and sprinted in the opposite direction. He dashed through the kitchen, slowing only to pull down a few food carts to throw obstacles into the course behind him.

The zombies scrambled after him. Some fell over the metal shelves and the ones on their heels crawled over them with ease. They closed in on Mead as he neared the rear exit.

He hit the metal door and slammed down the handle, but the door wouldn't open. He tried again with the same result.

"Shit!" He remembered the door needed to be unlocked and searched his pockets for his card.

Mead risked a glance back. The closest zombie was only yards away.

He found his key card and swiped it. The door unlocked. Mead thrust it open and fell out into the parking lot. He spun on his knees and shoved the door closed. He could hear the zombies hit the other side, pounding against it, but the heavy steel door held them back.

Just as he tried to catch his breath, he thought about the front entrance. With what little energy he had left, he ran around the building, grabbing his keys from his pocket and thanking God because the only reason he had them was because he was scheduled to close that night.

The front of the restaurant was clear. Mead slid his key into the lock and sealed the door tight. The creatures inside heard the click, and the few zombies which hadn't chased him all the way through the kitchen ran toward the door.

The first one there was Cindy, and Mead couldn't help but take a longing look as her breasts pressed against the smoked glass.

"What a waste."

The zombies beat their fists against the door, but they were trapped.

Mead backed away from the restaurant, toward employee parking. He pulled off his hair net, and his greasy hair tumbled to his shoulders.

He threw the net onto the pavement and climbed into his Cavalier. It started with a bang, and, as he drove away, he couldn't resist a glance at the huge "All You Can Eat" sign perched atop the roof.

"You're not eating me. Not today, anyway."

CHAPTER SIXTEEN

WIM'S FARM stood about twelve miles from the nearest town, and he only made the trip once or twice a month when he needed groceries or had to pick up parts for something that had broken down.

Calling it a town was a stretch. There was one stop light that marked the intersection of Elm and Main Street, and it turned into a blinker after 5 p.m. Along those roads were two bars, a gas station and sub shop, a market, and three churches along with rows of old, residential homes.

After killing Hoyt the mailman, Wim had decided that his only option was to go to town. The way he figured, there were two possible outcomes. Either everyone would be normal, and he'd be arrested for murder, or maybe lynched on the spot if he dared share his crazy story. Or, there would be more zombies. If the latter were to occur, he decided it was best to be prepared, so he loaded up his old Ford Bronco with every gun he had on the farm.

His father had been a collector, and, altogether, Wim found fourteen firearms. There were six rifles, two shotguns, four revolvers, and two pistols. He had ammunition for each, and Wim loaded them all to capacity, then put the remaining ammunition in the truck, just in case.

Wim didn't pass a living, or dead, soul on his way to town. The first building he came across was the post office. The small red brick structure stood a quarter mile outside of town, and when Wim turned into the parking lot, all the spaces were empty. In a village of less than a thousand, that wasn't an unusual sight. Since the man he'd earlier murdered was employed there, he figured it was as good a place to start as any.

Although he knew that it was a crime to take a firearm into a federal building, Wim grabbed a snub-nosed revolver that was small enough to fit into his pocket before he headed inside. Under the circumstances, he wasn't too worried about being a scofflaw.

Brass bells above the door jingled as he walked inside. All the lights were off and the lobby was empty.

"Hello?"

He walked to the counter and peered into the mail sorting area where he saw no one. Large bags of undelivered mail were strewn about the floor.

"Hello? Anyone here?"

Silence.

As he looked around, Wim noticed the cash register drawer was hanging open and filled with undisturbed money.

The eeriness of the situation was getting to him, and when a thunderous crash exploded outside, he jumped a good three inches in the air.

The sound had come from the rear of the building, so Wim hopped the counter, rushed through the mail room, and out the back door. As soon as he stepped into the daylight, he saw a pickup truck crashed into the back wall, its front end crumpled like an accordion. White smoke billowed from the crushed engine compartment.

Wim approached the driver's side and saw the door open, but the cab was empty. He wondered if everyone in the world had up and disappeared like in one of those *Twilight Zone* episodes his mother had always watched.

He moved around the truck and looked past it, and it was only then that he saw Nate Bauer, one of three brothers who owned a local contracting company. Nate was a loud, boisterous man who always had a juicy bit of gossip or an off-color joke to share, but today he wasn't laughing.

Nate sat on the road and gripped what looked like a red, wet rope. A few yards away from him was another man, an Amish pumpkin farmer who Wim recognized from the produce auctions but whose name he didn't know. That man clutched the other end of the rope.

"Mr. Bauer?" Wim called out.

Neither of the men reacted, so Wim approached them with caution. When he got within a few feet, he could see they weren't holding a rope. They were holding Nate Bauer's intestines.

Nate's plain, white button-down was scarlet with blood, and his guts protruded from a fist size gash in his belly. Nate held onto his intestines with both hands while the Amishman pulled in the other direction with all his strength. It was like they were in a life and death game of tug of war.

"Christ on the cross," Wim said. Despite what had happened on the farm, he still struggled to believe this was real.

Nate looked at him, his face pained and pale. "He's stealing my guts, Wim! Help me!"

Wim was frozen in place. He looked at the Amishman and saw his scraggly, gray beard was stained red.

"Kill him! Kill him or I'm gonna die," Nate said.

Wim broke out of his daze. He ran toward the Amishman.

"Let him go!" Wim said, trying to sound forceful, but he could hear the fear in his own voice even as he took out the pistol.

The Amishman ignored him and ripped a few more feet of Nate's insides to the outside. Nate bellowed in pain. Wim raised the revolver, aimed, and fired. The bullet zipped through the air, and part of the Amishman's right ear hopped off his head like a jumping bean.

The man tumbled over sideways and dropped the intestines. Nate pulled them back in, like he was collecting an unraveled extension cord.

The Amishman dove for the guts but missed. Then he turned toward Wim. His eyes were blank and dead, and he was missing a chunk of flesh on his cheek.

The man grabbed hold of Wim's left leg and chomped down on his calf. Even through the heavy denim of his jeans, Wim could feel the power of the bite.

Wim kicked out, and his heavy boot caught the Amishman in the midsection and knocked him onto his back.

"Kill him!" Nate screamed.

Wim glanced toward Nate and saw that he was trying to push his intestines, which were covered with dirt and shale and grass, back through the hole in his belly.

As he looked away, the Amishman grabbed Wim from behind. He caught his fingers in Wim's belt and pulled him down. Wim fell on top of him, his back against the zombie's front.

He heard the dead man's jaws snapping and tried to keep his head raised up. With every attempted bite, the zombie was closer to getting him, and Wim could feel spittle hitting the exposed nape of his neck.

Wim threw his elbow back once and then again, both times catching the zombie in the stomach. He did it a third time, heard a rib break, and the zombie released him.

He rolled free of it and onto his knees. As the zombie sat up, Wim was ready, and he shot it in the face. A dime-sized hole appeared under his left eye, and he fell backward.

Wim quickly crawled away from it, horrified by the situation. He caught his breath, then checked his leg where he'd been bitten. There was a white outline on his skin, but the zombie's teeth hadn't penetrated his jeans or his flesh. Then Wim looked to Nate Bauer, who was lying motionless on his side. He'd managed to get about half his guts back into his stomach, but nonetheless, Nate was dead.

Wim sat down in the street, ran his fingers through his black hair, and wondered again how this could be real. There were no such things as zombies. That's just made-up movie nonsense meant to scare kids and sell popcorn. But if it was made up, then what in the world had just happened?

And then Nate Bauer groaned.

Wim looked and saw the man's eyes were open, but like the Amishman and the mailman before him, they were blank. Slowly, Nate's head turned, first looking left and then to the right where Wim sat.

When he saw Wim, the zombie rolled onto his stomach and crawled to his knees. His guts fell back out the gash, and when he made it to his feet and staggered toward Wim, his intestines dragged on the ground behind him.

Wim jumped to his feet and backed away. Nate kept coming toward him. He growled and bared his teeth like a rabid animal.

Wim raised the gun, but just as he pulled the trigger, the zombie stepped on his own intestines and fell forward. His face hit the pavement with a crunching thud. Before it could get up, Wim put a round in the back of its skull.

When Wim looked up from the lifeless body, he saw that the gunfire had drawn a small crowd. Seven zombies, all people he knew, staggered toward him. He retraced his path through the post office and returned to his truck. More zombies had arrived on Main Street, too.

The world is cursed, Wim thought. He couldn't understand why this had happened and, even more confusingly, why he was left alive. Maybe he was the cursed one. Why was he more worthy of life than all of these good people? Why was he spared? Why was he the one left to clean up? He almost wished he would have just died right along with his pigs and chickens.

He removed the guns from the Bronco and lined them up on the hood. Once he'd laid them all out for easy access, he took the Marlin 336 that he used for hunting deer and leaned against the side of the Bronco for stability.

One of the zombies was Dale Yoder, who owned the greenhouse where Wim bought his tomato plants every spring. Wim lined up the peep sights of the Marlin with Dale's head and pulled the trigger. This was going to be a long day.

CHAPTER SEVENTEEN

RAMEY'S TEXTS and calls to Loretta had gone unanswered for almost five hours. Most days, that wouldn't be enough to garner a raised eyebrow, but the world had gone to hell, and that changed everything.

It seemed like the entire town was sick. Well, almost everyone. Ramey was fine, but the way Loretta was hacking and coughing around, never bothering to cover her mouth or wash her hands, the girl knew it was only a matter of time before she caught whatever germs had taken up residence in their crummy trailer.

Since the power went out, most of the trailer park residents had moved outside, where they grilled whatever meat they had before it could spoil. Through the thin walls of the mobile home, Ramey could hear the steady drone of country music accompanied by a chorus of coughing and sneezing. It was like the Fourth of July in a tuberculosis hospital.

While the rest of the park celebrated, Ramey retreated to her room and tried to ignore everything. Today, she sat on her bed and unfolded the last letter her father had sent. It had arrived in the mail over a year ago. His words, in his neat, blocky print, were few.

Ramey,

Please join me.

It's safe here.

I promise.

Dad

He included a map and a phone number. Ramey never called the number or responded to the letter. Now, the phones were all out of service, and it was too late. Not that it mattered. Whatever was happening here in northern New York was probably happening wherever he was, too.

She heard the trailer door bang open.

"Ramey!" Loretta called out in a gravely rumble.

Ramey absent-mindedly shoved the letter into her pocket as she left her bedroom. By the time she got to the living room (and in a forty-foot-long trailer, that was a short trip), Loretta had already crashed on the couch.

Loretta's eyes were sleepy and so bloodshot they looked like she'd been crying blood. She turned her head when she heard Ramey's footsteps.

"Isss terrible ou' there."

Ramey sat down at the computer desk and stared at her mother. "I know. And you disappear for half a day. Thanks, Mom."

"Had to get something."

Loretta squeezed a plastic baggie she held in her hand. Ramey noticed. She wanted to scream, to tell her mother she was a waste of a life. To tell her she was an awful mother. To tell her she should have left with her dad. But she didn't. She'd yelled and cried and tried to reason with Loretta thousands of times, but the way the drugs made her feel was more important than anything Ramey had to say, so she said nothing.

"This is for us." Loretta held out the bag, which included crystal meth and a chunk of black tar heroin.

Ramey stared in disbelief. "Have you lost your mind?"

Loretta tried to sit up but only managed to half slump against the armrest. "You don't understand. Isss the end of the world."

Loretta coughed up a mouthful of blood. She looked at the red spittle in her palm, then to her daughter. "I'm dying, Ramey. Everyone out there's dying, but they don't stay dead."

Ramey wondered what hallucinogens her mother had ingested prior to returning home with this buffet of dope. Loretta was at the stage in her addiction where she would take anything if it was cheap or free.

"What are you talking about?"

"You remember Henry Geary?"

Ramey did. Mr. Geary owned Hank's, a local pizza joint that everyone in town knew was a front for his real business of selling drugs. It was the same restaurant where Bobby Mack bought the marijuana they smoked before their two minutes of passion.

"He died last night. Everyone knows it. But this morning, I seen him walking around inside the restaurant, so I went up to that big glass window and looked inside, and, Ramey, he was eating his wife. Eating her!"

Loretta went through another painful coughing fit, and Ramey thought she might pass out. She moved to get up, but Loretta recovered and waved at her to stay seated.

"He snot the only one, either. I saw it happening in the alley behind the drug store, too. I tried to tell people, but no one believed me. Isss like it says in the bible. 'When Hell's full, the dead will walk the Earth.'"

"That's not from the bible, Mom."

Loretta ignored her and opened her bag o' drugs. "I got this so we can just go to sleep. We can go to sleep and not have to hurt no more. There's been too mush hurtin' a'ready."

Ramey saw the sincerity in Loretta's eyes. This might have been the first honest thing her mother had said to her in years. The irony that Loretta's best mothering came in suggesting they commit double suicide wasn't lost on her. She moved to her mother and laid her hand over Loretta's drug-filled fist.

"You don't have to do this. I'll throw this out. Then, I'll go to the hospital and get you actual medicine, and you'll be okay."

Loretta's eyes blazed fierce, and she jerked her hand free of Ramey's. She clutched the drugs against her deflated bosom like they were the golden ring and she was Gollum.

"You ain't taking 'em from me! Don't you dare!"

Ramey's temporary compassion vanished. This cold, shrewish woman huddled on the couch wasn't a mother. She was barely a human being.

"Okay. Do what you want, but leave me alone."

Ramey retreated to her room and locked the door behind her. She didn't know if Loretta would actually overdose, and, much to her own relief, she no longer cared.

CHAPTER EIGHTEEN

THE CHOPPER SOARED through the air for over an hour, and, the whole time, Miller hadn't spoken another word. Mitch stared out the window as they flew. They passed over cities and suburbs, but for the most recent leg of the voyage, he'd seen nothing but trees and mountains. He'd never had much of a sense of direction and could get disoriented in shopping malls, so he didn't know if they were heading north, south, east, or west. He wondered if they might have flown to Canada. Wasn't Canada just a bunch of trees and nothingness?

As the helicopter dropped in elevation, Mitch noticed a small town coming in to view below them. Town wasn't even the right word for it. Maybe village would do. It looked to consist of a single street and some buildings.

"Where are we?" he dared ask.

Miller looked back at him for the first time since they departed the Marsten Academy. He removed his sunglasses and yellow-green pus seeped from the corners of the soldier's eyes. It reminded Mitch of the time he had pinkeye in third grade, but about a thousand times worse.

"The Greenbriar," Miller said.

"What's that?"

Miller coughed into his elbow and smiled. It was the most horrible smile Mitch had ever seen in his life. He imagined that's how the Grim Reaper would look when he came to collect your soul and snuff out your candle.

"That's your safe zone, kid. Where all the little rich pricks like you get to hide out until hell blows over."

Mitch couldn't look at him anymore and returned his attention to the ground below. A sprawling white building came into view. A bizarre marriage of limousines and Humvees filled the parking lot. He noticed more helicopters, both coming in for landings and taking off.

The chopper touched down on the roof. Mitch unbuckled and waited for Miller to give him the go-ahead. When the copter settled, the soldier cocked his thumb toward the exit.

Mitch moved to the door. The step down was a big one, and Miller emoted something that sounded like a wet, thick laugh. "Need a hand?"

He extended his palm, but Mitch shook his head and jumped out.

The whirling propeller turned his long, brown hair into a bird's nest. He took a step away, but a hot hand caught the back of his jacket.

Miller hissed into his ear. "I hope every one of you rots."

Mitch pulled himself free, and the chopper flew up and away. He thought he could still feel Miller's sticky breath on his neck and was desperate for a shower. As he tried to shake off the willies, a fit man in a black suit and sunglasses jogged toward him. Secret Service; Mitch could tell with barely a glance.

"Chapman?" His voice was tight and controlled. Mitch nodded. "Come with me. And welcome to the Greenbrier."

———

THEY TOOK AN ELEVATOR RIDE DOWN FROM THE ROOF, AND MITCH thought the plunge would last forever. The agent never tendered his name and made no attempt at small talk. When the elevator stopped, the doors opened to reveal a long corridor, which looked straight out of the seventies with bright, orange and red seizure-inducing wallpaper.

"This way." The agent led him down the hall, the walk so long and brisk that Mitch struggled to catch his breath. He wished he hadn't taken the Valium. Or that he had more coke. Or, better yet, both.

At the end of the corridor, it seemed they'd reached a dead end, but the agent grabbed onto the wall, and the next thing Mitch knew, it unfolded like an accordion, and behind it stood a massive stainless steel door. The man then tapped a series of numbers into a keypad. Unseen gears whirled and rotated, and the silver door popped open.

The agent swung it outward, and Mitch saw the reverse side had a round handle that you could turn to open and close it from the inside, the kind of mechanisms they had on submarines or bank vaults. Inside was a second, identical door. The agent repeated his keypad trick and opened it. This one was even thicker, two feet deep, and even the fit agent seemed to struggle against the weight of it.

Once opened, it revealed a room decorated with red checked wall-paper and black and white floor tiles. Dozens of people in suits and dresses filled the space. To Mitch, it looked like something out of the party scene in *The Shining*, but he had no time to take in the surround-ings before his mother burst from the crowd and wrapped him up in a stifling embrace. Mitch couldn't remember for sure the last time she'd hugged him like that but was certain he could still count out his age on one hand when it had happened.

"Mitchell, thank God. Thank God you made it." A statuesque, lithe woman, Margaret Chapmen was taller than Mitch, and her breasts pressed awkwardly into his face as she held him. He didn't pull away.

He found comfort in her grip and felt much younger than his sixteen years.

"You're smothering the boy, Margaret." It was his father's curt voice, and, at the sound of it, his mother let loose. Mitchell looked over to see his father, clad in his trademark navy blue suit, examining him. The man was pushing sixty now, but his hair was still black with only hints of gray speckled throughout. His emotionless face was mostly void of wrinkles—certainly no laugh lines—with only a deep cut between his brows to make him look more like a man than a mannequin.

"You look well, Mitchell."

They hadn't seen each other in several months, and Mitch knew his haircut would have garnered a lecture under normal circumstances, but this was not normal. "So do you."

His father put his hand on his shoulder. "We need to take you to admissions."

"What's that?"

His father didn't answer.

———

THE FIRST STOP WAS AN EXAMINATION BY A TEAM OF DOCTORS. THEY took his temperature (98.1 degrees) and blood pressure (115 over 74). They shined lights into his eyes, ears, and up his nose. And at the end, a beefy male nurse with a rose tattoo on his forearm stuck a fat, gloved index finger up Mitch's narrow asshole without bothering to lube up first. Even Rochelle had never gone there. Afterward, someone took his photo, and a few moments later, he had a new ID badge.

Soldiers led Mitch to a room that was mercifully void of wallpaper. Double-decker bunk beds filled the cavernous space.

A soldier posted at the door pointed at one of the bunks. "That's yours."

"What about my parents?"

"You'll receive nightly briefings."

The soldier turned away from him, and Mitch surveyed the room. A few men occupied bunks, but it was more empty than full. Mitch sat on the edge of his bed, and a guy in his twenties with spiked blonde hair nodded at him. He looked somewhat familiar.

"I'm Thad Winebruner. You're Chapman's kid, right?"

Mitch vaguely remembered that Winebruner had been in trouble a few months earlier. Drinking and driving, or maybe it was public intoxication. Mitch's father had informed him of the situation and had added, "His father probably won't win his next election because of him," and gave Mitch a look that said, 'Don't you dare ruin my career, boy.'

"Mitch," he said and extended his hand, and Winebruner shook it. The blond's palm was moist and his grip weak. "Is your dad here?" Mitch asked.

"Yeah. They have a huge room where they can hold a joint session of Congress. The show must go on and all that shit."

"Do you know what's going on?"

Winebruner shook his head. "Not really. I've heard rumors. Mostly about some crazy bad flu that's killing everybody who gets it. But some other shit, too."

"Like what?"

Winebruner motioned Mitch toward him. Mitch stepped to his bunk, and Winebruner glanced around the room to make sure they weren't being watched. He leaned in close to Mitch and spoke in a hissing whisper.

"Zombie shit!"

Mitch flinched backward. "You're screwing with me."

Winebruner shrugged his shoulders. "Believe me or don't. No skin off my nose."

The young man flopped back on his mattress and thumbed through a seventies edition of *Hustler*, leaving Mitch alone with his thoughts.

He'd always hated being a senator's son, but apparently, it had benefits after all. It didn't seem fair they got to hole up in some mega-complex, safe from whatever bug was killing people, but there was an old saying about gift horses, and Mitch wasn't about to turn down a safe haven.

He heard someone a few bunks down sneeze. Has to be a coincidence, that's all. Nevertheless, when he looked down at his arms, he saw the fine, dark hairs all standing at attention.

CHAPTER NINETEEN

BLOOD LEAKED from the ear canal, trickled over the tragus, and down the earlobe, where it formed fat, wet drops that plunged onto the white floor. The way the puddle grew reminded Solomon of that old monster movie, *The Blob*, and he half thought it might rise off the floor and attack him. Wendy's vengeance come to life.

He knew as long as his wife kept bleeding; she was alive, but it had been almost four hours since he welcomed her home by slamming the crescent wrench into the back of her head. He dragged her limp body from the foyer to the kitchen, then sat her upright in a chair and waited for her to come to. Doubts about whether that was going to happen filled his mind with worry. Not because he was afraid she would die. She had that coming. But first, Wendy needed to know what she'd done to him.

He'd loved the bitch since he was seventeen and she was fourteen. She was the daughter of a local barrister, and he a street thug more likely to end up in prison than attend university. It took him a good four months to convince her to go out with him, but when she did, he refused to let go.

Despite what many would have thought from looking at him, Solomon could be a charmer when he wanted. Sometimes, it was that charm that kept Wendy at his side. Other times, she stayed out of fear. He didn't care why she stayed as long as she did.

He knew she'd whored around on him in the past. Once, he caught her drawers down in their Birmingham loft, riding a university lad like he was a polo pony. After he beat the boy into a coma in front of her, he packed her a bag, and they were on a jet to the U.S. She promised to never do it again. He believed her. And if there was one thing Solomon Baldwin hated more than a lying slag, it was being wrong.

Remembering her lies and whoring brought the anger flooding through him like water through a broken dam. He grabbed a fistful of her bloody hair and jerked her head up. Her eyes remained closed and her mouth fell ajar, allowing pink-tinged drool to dribble out in a slimy rope. He recalled that she'd had a cold the last few days, blowing her nose nonstop and sounding like a goose with the plague.

"Wakey wakey, love. Time to come around and take your medicine."

She didn't react. He released her head and let it drop down. Her chin hit her chest, and her mouth snapped shut so hard the sound of it made Solomon's teeth hurt. The sound also gave him an idea.

He leaned in close to her ear, his lips drawn back in a skeletal grin. "If you're faking, love, best to stop right quick."

Solomon waited a moment and got no reaction. Then, he pressed his face against the side of her head and took her earlobe between his teeth. He bit down fast and hard. Her blood gushed into his mouth. Hot, wet pennies.

He swallowed a mouthful of it, then clenched his jaws tight as a vise and felt her skin give away as the bottom part of her ear separated from her body. The nickel-sized lump of flesh fell into his mouth and laid on his tongue like a wad of used-up chewing gum. He spat it free, and it bounced twice when it hit the tile.

Through it all, Wendy didn't move.

Christ, I must have really scrambled her eggs.

He took his thumb and forefinger and opened her right eyelid. The white sclera had gone red. Not the roadmap of red veins like he'd seen in his drunk of a father's eyes growing up, either—it was completely crimson, like her entire eyeball was filled with blood instead of whatever goo was supposed to be inside. Solomon screwed up his mouth in shock and disgust, then checked her other eye and found the same.

Solomon crossed to the cabinet under the sink, opened it, and removed a bottle of ammonia. He wished he had smelling salts, but if there was any chance of her coming back around, this would do just as well. He popped off the plastic cap and stepped back to his wife.

Solomon held the bottle a few inches away from her face and waited. Nothing. He raised it up so that it touched her nose. She groaned.

This was what he'd been waiting for. "There we go, love. Come back now to the land of the living."

Wendy groaned again. It didn't sound like pain. The sound came from deeper inside, from somewhere far down in her diaphragm. It sounded almost inhuman. Solomon didn't realize it, but he took a step back.

Wendy raised her head up, and as she did, more of the pink ooze dripped from her mouth. Her eyelids fluttered. Solomon could see her eyeballs darting back and forth beneath the thin layer of tissue. Another groan reverberated from her mouth, and when it faded to an end, her eyes opened.

Solomon studied her as she looked around the room. Confused? No, vacant. He took a step toward her, back in arm's reach, and when he did so, her eyes locked on him. *You see me now, don't you?*

Almost as if she'd read his thoughts, Wendy unleashed a pained cough that sent red spittle flying from her mouth. It splashed against his face, and, for a moment, he stood there, too surprised to react. And in that half-second pause, Wendy was on her feet.

Solomon snapped out of his momentary daze when he saw her diving at him, her crazed face closing in on his own. He realized he still clutched the ammonia bottle, and he smashed the jug across her face. She stumbled backward, and he squeezed the plastic, sending a geyser of ammonia into her face.

The momentarily blinded Wendy clawed at her sightless eyes. Her perfectly manicured nails ripped streaks of flesh from her cheeks. Solomon thought they looked like unrolled streamers dangling from her face. Solomon knew she was no longer his wife. She was a monster.

Bugger me.

She sprinted at him, crossing the kitchen in an instant. Solomon threw the empty jug, and it bounced off her head harmlessly. She dove at him, growling as she did, and hit him in the chest. He stumbled back, tripping over a chair and crashing to the floor.

His head smacked against the tile and everything went black for a moment. When his vision returned, he saw a galaxy of stars, but amid the constellations was Wendy's snarling, crazed face.

She was on all fours, crouching on top of him like a wild dog. When he saw the bloody saliva frothing from her lips, he realized she was not a pissed-off housewife.

The bird's gone rabid.

Almost on cue, she tried to bite him. Her mouth was on a collision course with his nose, but he swung his right fist upward and nailed her square in the throat. He felt something crunch as his hand connected with her flesh and drove deep into her neck.

The Wendy-thing coughed—shrill, whiny whistling noises that puffed out small mists of blood. Solomon rolled onto his side and sent her toppling off of him. He punched her again, this time smashing her nose flat and knocking her onto her back.

Solomon jumped up and ran out of the kitchen, dashing through the dining room and into the foyer, where an antique buffet stood against the wall. He heard Wendy's footsteps thundering behind him as he fumbled with the drawer, yanking it sideways and jamming it. Open up, you bastard!

She was close enough he could hear her choking, wheezing coughs. He guessed he had five seconds at the most and jerked the drawer with all his strength. Wood cracked and splintered as the drawer gave way and revealed the object he'd been looking for: a generic black pistol. One thing Solomon loved about America was how damned easy it was to buy guns.

He snatched the pistol and spun on his heels. Wendy was almost on top of him. He raised the gun and fired off a round. It slammed into the center of her chest, just above where the deep gash of her ample cleavage began. A black dot appeared, and his wife, or whatever she'd become, stumbled backward a step.

But she didn't go down.

The gunshot only seemed to enrage her more. She snapped her jaws and moved toward him again.

She's a fucking zombie!

He aimed the gun at her again and shot a second round. That one punched a hole high on her forehead at her hairline. The bullet tore a channel through the top of her skull, sending bone and hair and blood flying. Wendy crumpled to the ground, the top of her head cleaved in two. Motionless at last.

Solomon took a step toward her and straddled her lifeless body as he stared down on her. He felt energized, almost high. Then he aimed the pistol and fired another bullet through her face.

"Not so pretty anymore, are ya, love?"

Wendy didn't answer.

He could hear a siren in the far distance, but that didn't alarm him. If his wife had indeed turned into a zombie, the police had much bigger issues to worry about than his dead whore of a wife. So did he.

Solomon returned to the broken buffet, grabbed a handful of bullets, and reloaded the pistol. He deposited the remaining ammunition into his pocket. He didn't bother to take in his reflection in the mirror on the wall. If he had, the fact that he was covered in blood wouldn't have stopped him from going outside. There was work to be done, and he was more than willing to get his hands dirty.

CHAPTER TWENTY

ABEN'S LIPS stuck to his teeth, his tongue to the roof of his mouth. It was like he'd dined on a seven-course meal of cotton. A few hours earlier, he had checked the toilet. Old pubic hair and calcified piss decorated the rim. The bowl was stained brown, and the water carried a strong aroma of iron mixed with stale puke. He decided he'd rather be thirsty.

The beginnings of sunlight brightened the room, and Aben could see the clock on the wall showed ten minutes after six when he heard the door to the building bang open, then close. He assumed it was the relief officer, but when the source of the pounding footsteps appeared in the office, he saw it was Dolan.

The officer's eyes were feverish and bloodshot but also appeared hyper-alert. He wore gray sweatpants and a white thermal shirt, which had ridden up over his bulbous, vein-streaked belly. A beer drinker's gut, Aben thought. It was hard to tell for sure in the dim light of dawn, but Aben thought he saw specks of red against the white cotton material. Dolan also held his pistol.

"Is Ken here yet?"

"Who?" Aben asked.

"Ken Irwin. The other officer."

Aben waved his hand as if displaying the empty room. "No one here but me. And you, now."

Dolan flopped into the chair behind the desk and grabbed the phone. He listened, tapped the receiver then tossed down the handset. He stood and paced back and forth, still clutching the gun. Aben could see there were, in fact, red specks on Dolan's shirt, and as he tried to discern whether or not they were blood, Dolan stopped pacing and looked straight at him.

"I just killed my wife." His voice was flat and matter of fact, like he was describing taking out the garbage. Aben thought he must have heard wrong.

"You what?"

"She was sick. Like everyone else."

As if on cue, Dolan sneezed. Aben could see the small droplets of spittle propel through the air. The sun backlit them, and it looked like a storm of millions of dust particles raining down.

"When I got home last night, she was sick but okay. We ate leftovers and went to bed. Then I woke up because she was having some kind of fit, shaking all over and foaming at the mouth, and her skin was hot as a hot water bottle. And then she just died."

"I thought you said you killed her."

Dolan paced again. His voice became more anxious as he continued on. "She died. I tried to call for an ambulance, but the phone was dead. So, I went next door to the neighbor's for help, but no one came to the door."

Dolan looked out the office's only window and gazed onto the empty street. "I went back home and sat down on the bed beside her, and I held her hand because I didn't know what else to do."

Aben looked again to the red on Dolan's shirt and knew the story wasn't over. Soon enough, the telling of it recommenced.

"I was still holding her hand when..." He paused, opened his mouth to speak, then closed it again.

Aben had seen the haunted, self-loathing look on Dolan's face before. After an exceptionally dirty battle or a raid in which women or children were killed. He even wore it himself a time or two.

"Then she came back."

"She woke up?"

"No. She wasn't asleep. She was dead. She was dead, and then she came back. She turned over in bed and looked at me and... and she grabbed my arm and tried to bite me. I screamed, 'Helen! What are you doing?' but it was like she didn't hear me at all. She just kept trying to bite me."

Aben saw the horrified sincerity in Dolan's eyes, and it almost convinced him to believe the insane story the cop was telling.

"I pushed her off me, and she fell off the bed, but right away she got back up and came after me again. I kept screaming, 'Stop! Stop! Stop!' but she didn't stop."

"I had my service pistol on the nightstand." He held up the gun and talked to it instead of Aben. "I told her to stop one more time, but she wouldn't. So, I shot her. I shot her right in the chest. But that didn't stop her, either. So, I shot her again. And again. And she just kept coming after me. So I shot her in the head."

He looked back to Aben. "And then she died again."

Dolan raised the gun, and, for a split second, Aben thought the cop would shoot him, too. Instead, Dolan pressed the silver barrel into the soft, pale flesh under his jaw.

"No! Don't!" Aben shouted, but it was too late.

Dolan squeezed the trigger, and the top part of his head blew off like a party popper on New Year's Eve. Only instead of expelling miniature confetti, this one unleashed blood and brains and bone. The wet mess hit the low ceiling with an audible thwack. Most fell back to the floor, but a few bits remained behind, clinging to the white tile like gory graffiti.

Dolan crumpled to his knees, then fell backward in a lifeless heap. From his viewpoint on the toilet, Aben could see the gaping hole in the top of his skull. Pints of blood gushed from the wound and from Dolan's mouth, forming abstract patterns over the concrete floor.

Aben had seen men die before. He'd seen the aftermath, too. So the gruesomeness of the situation wasn't shocking. What bothered him far more than the gore was what Dolan had said before he cashed in his chips.

Did his wife come back from the dead, then try to attack him? To eat him? The idea was so insane that Aben half believed it. He looked again to the clock on the wall and counted down the minutes until the relief officer was due to arrive.

CHAPTER TWENTY-ONE

AFTER RUNNING FOR SEVERAL MILES, Bolivar's lungs were on fire and he struggled to keep up with his younger and fitter colleagues. Sawyer was far ahead, shooting every zombie that got too close. The most recent was a city police officer who still wore his navy blue service cap even though his nose had been bitten clean off his face. Sawyer put a bullet in his forehead.

Peduto noticed Jorge falling behind. "Come on. Almost there."

They had picked up two new arrivals as they weaved around and between buildings. The first was a man who looked about fifty and wore a faded Lenny Dykstra Phillies' jersey decorated with twenty-five years' worth of beer, nacho, and relish stains. The second was a boy who appeared to be no more than thirteen, yet kept a hand cannon tucked into the waistband of his baggy jeans. In the rush, no one had bothered to get their names.

The five of them were now only a few blocks from the Wells Fargo Center, the former home of the Flyers and 76ers. The military had commandeered the arena at the beginning of the outbreak and turned it into their headquarters and residence for more than fifteen thousand personnel.

Everything was clear as they ran down tree-lined Broad Street, but when they came to the intersection of Zinkoff Boulevard, they ran into more than twenty zombies feasting on six dead soldiers. When the zombies saw the quintet, half broke off and gave chase.

Fresh fear gave Bolivar a second wind, and he caught up to the others. As the arena came into view, he saw hundreds of military vehicles filling the acres of the parking lot. As far as Bolivar could see, all were empty. They sprinted across the concrete until they reached the entrance at the front of the Center.

The boy was at the head of the pack, ten yards ahead of Sawyer, who was shockingly fast for a man of his size. The kid bounced off the smoked glass doors when they didn't open.

"What the fuck, man? They're locked!" the kid yelled. He looked back to the others and to the zombies behind them. "You said we'd be safe here!"

Sawyer closed the gap. Peduto wasn't far behind, and Bolivar was on his heels. He could see chains and a padlock holding the doors shut. What none of them saw, until it was too late, was the kid drawing the cannon from his waistband. He pressed the muzzle against the lock.

"Don't!" Sawyer screamed. He was only a few feet away now, but that was still too far to intervene.

The kid was either pulling the trigger already or didn't care to listen. The gun thundered, and the padlock blew into pieces, which clattered to the cement walkway. After pulling away the now loose chains, the kid yanked open the double doors.

"Mother of God." The words came out of Sawyer's mouth at an abnormally low volume. Maybe he didn't even realize he'd said them aloud. All of his attention was focused on the area behind the now open doors.

The kid turned back to Sawyer and didn't see what was coming. He picked the wrong time to listen.

"What?" he asked, and with his attention diverted, he was clueless to the sea of zombies ebbing toward him until they grabbed him and dragged him into the building.

The zombies packed the arena in standing-room-only fashion. It was impossible to see anything but the living dead inside.

Several of them clawed at the kid's head while others pulled at his arms, legs, and torso. Some bit and ate and swallowed as others fought for their piece of the pie. The kid screamed, and when he opened his mouth, zombie fingers filled the cavity. They tugged and strained until the flesh and tendons gave way.

His right cheek went first, tearing like papier-mâché all the way to his ear. Next, his entire lower jaw ripped free from his skull. The zombie that secured that prize was an Army nurse, her uniform ripped and bloody. She raised the jawbone to her mouth and chewed off the boy's skin like she was eating a rack of ribs.

Somehow, the kid kept screaming. With nothing to hold it in place, his tongue swung back and forth like a pendulum on a clock. At least, it did until a zombie soldier leaned in and bit it clean off.

Sawyer leveled his M4 carbine and put the kid out of his misery. "Back! Go back!" Sawyer ordered.

The zombies poured out of the arena as fast as they could funnel through the open doors. Dozens turned into scores which became hundreds and then thousands, all in less than a minute.

CHAPTER TWENTY-TWO

TRAFFIC CREPT along at fifteen miles an hour as they approached the tunnel. Emory steered into the passing lane, but it did little good. He glanced over at Christopher, who slumped to the side, his sweaty forehead making a hazy oil slick against the passenger side window.

Within minutes after hitting the road, Emory realized that Christopher, the boy so concerned about his aunt, was, in fact, very sick himself. His breaths came slow and shallow, and it sounded as if his lungs were full of mucous. He couldn't last more than a few minutes in between coughing spells, and his skin felt like hot embers. Emory guessed his temperature to be well over a hundred and climbing.

Overhead, an LED traffic alert sign flashed, "Backups expected at the tunnel. Drive Carefully," and as they passed underneath it, a bright yellow motorcycle zipped between both lanes and came within inches of clipping cars on each side. That only slowed traffic down even more.

It took another five minutes to go the last mile, but once they reached the tunnel, traffic opened up, and speeds quadrupled.

Emory had driven the Mercedes a hundred yards into the tunnel when Christopher broke out in uncontrollable coughs. The boy gasped for air, choking. He searched for the seatbelt release, desperate.

"Can't... breathe..." He unbuckled the belt and leaned into the dash, holding his chest as thick, tight coughs racked his body.

"Hold on, Christopher. We're getting there."

The boy's coughing ceased, but Emory's relief was short lived as Christopher fell back into the seat in convulsions. Bloody foam oozed from his mouth, and his head snapped back and forth so violently Emory thought the boy would give himself whiplash.

He looked away from Christopher just in time to see the yellow motorcycle discarded on the road in front of him. It was too late to hit the brakes, and the Mercedes hit the bike at almost seventy miles an hour.

The car careened sideways, and the front left wheel caught the narrow raised walkway at the edge of the tunnel. It climbed the concrete, the driver's side now two feet off the road, and then it rolled.

Emory had felt nothing so forceful in his entire life. He thought every joint in his body was tearing apart. The roar of the crash deafened his ears. The airbag burst in his face, knocking away his glasses and blinding him in a cloud of white powder.

The Mercedes crashed down onto its roof and slid twenty yards, sparks arcing as the metal scraped the pavement. The windows imploded and sent safety glass raining through the interior.

In a confused blur, Emory saw Christopher fly out the open cavity where the windshield had been. The boy disappeared as the car skidded away.

The momentum slowed, and Emory thought the crash might be over, but squealing brakes screamed behind him. He couldn't turn to look, and that was just as well because all he'd have seen was the huge blue bus barreling down on him.

The bus slammed into the Mercedes' back end and sent the car spinning like a top. Emory closed his eyes and waited to die.

But he didn't. The car stopped moving, and, this time, nothing else hit it. He looked around and saw smoke, which had taken on the puke green color of the fluorescent lights that illuminated the abyss of the two-mile-long tunnel.

Between the crash and being suspended upside down from the seatbelt, Emory struggled to get his bearings. He heard people screaming in the near distance and remembered Christopher.

Emory fumbled with the belt release, found the button, and braced himself with his other hand as he unlocked the belt. He half fell, half eased himself onto the roof of the car, and then crawled on his belly out the void left behind in the windshield.

Emory felt like his head was underwater and found it hard to think. He extended his arms which seemed to work as expected, then climbed onto his knees, then to his feet.

He ached. Every inch of his body felt battered and bruised, but nothing serious was broken. When he'd bought the Mercedes at his dearly departed Grant's insistence, the cost seemed downright obscene. Now, he realized its tank-like build had saved his life.

Pieces of broken vehicles littered the roadway. The acrid smoke burned his nose and made his eyes water, clouding his vision as he tiptoed around the wreckage and searched for Christopher.

Emory spotted the biker's bright yellow jacket first. He stumbled along the road toward Emory, but the closer he got, the odder he appeared. Emory saw the legs, the torso, and the arms, but nothing above the shoulders. It looked like a beheaded Frankenstein lurching at him.

As it got closer, Emory moved to the side and then saw the biker did have a head, one that still wore a helmet. But the head bent backward so far that it hung down between his shoulder blades.

"Oh, God in Heaven," Emory said as he took in that impossible sight.

He stepped toward the biker as it stumbled around blindly. He reached out and touched the helmet, which was painted to look like Pac Man. At the touch, the biker lurched toward him.

"I'll help you. Just stay still." Dear God, how is this man alive, he wondered.

Emory reached out and lifted the smoked glass face shield, careful to not twist or turn what must be a broken neck. What he discovered was the face of a dead man. The biker's lifeless eyes rolled in their sockets to see Emory. A muffled growl escaped its mouth, and Emory could hear the teeth clicking together.

The biker reached toward Emory in a wide, uncoordinated swing. Emory shoved it backward, and the zombie tripped over a piece of a bumper and fell onto the road.

When it hit, its head snapped up into a somewhat normal position. Then it climbed back to its feet, and the zombie's detached cranium wobbled on the neck in a way that reminded Emory of the way the old magicians would spin bowls and plates on sticks on the Ed Sullivan show.

Emory ran from the biker and into the putrid, green smoke that had filled the tunnel like a heavy fog.

"Christopher!" he called out, dashing around the fog in a fruitless search. "Christopher, where are you?"

He paused, listening for a vocal response. Instead, what he heard were the soles of shoes scraping against the pavement. That, and a cacophony of low groans.

Emory looked into the smoke, straining to see more than a few feet beyond his nose. He moved forward. Stopped. Then took a step backward.

Through the green haze, he could see movement. Human shapes walking, no, lurching toward him. Their awkward locomotion was not unlike that of the bobble-headed biker he'd just encountered. As they pushed through the smoke, Emory saw them in more detail.

Leading the way was a woman in a blue pantsuit with a jagged shard of metal sticking out of her left breast. A young boy who was missing an arm followed. Next came a beefy man in a trucker hat whose intestines sagged from a gash in his gut. Other zombies joined the parade.

Amongst them, he saw Christopher. The teen dragged himself along the road with his hands. His spine was twisted horribly askew, and his legs turned one hundred eighty degrees in the opposite direction.

"Oh, Christopher. I'm so sorry."

Emory wasn't even aware he'd said the words aloud, but the zombies heard him and turned almost in unison toward him and shuffled forward in their slow but unrelenting gait.

He took one more look into Christopher's dead eyes. The boy opened his mouth in a raspy growl and swatted at the air between them. Then he continued his soldier-styled belly crawl as fast as his dead arms could drag him.

Emory turned and ran and didn't stop. He hadn't run in years, but adrenaline carried him through the one plus mile of darkness until he could see the pinprick of light at the other end.

The brightness increased as he neared the exit, and Emory risked a glance behind him. He'd gained ground on the zombies, but they were still coming. He recalled the fable of the tortoise and the hare and realized they might never stop. That he'd have to keep running for the rest of his life.

As he closed in on the exit, the brilliant white light of day pained his eyes which had become accustomed to the dark, but he didn't slow down. Another fifty feet, and he burst into the daylight and into the city.

A labyrinth of highways and bridges stretched out ahead of him, and it took him a moment to understand why it seemed so foreign. Pittsburgh was almost empty. A handful of cars and trucks drove about, and a few dozen people walked to and fro, but it was a far cry from the bustling city he'd expect on a normal weekday afternoon.

"What the hell happened to you, Mister?"

Emory turned to look at a young man, maybe twenty, sucking on one of those electronic cigarettes that everyone seemed to use now. His curly blond hair blew into his eyes, and he pushed it away as he stared at Emory.

Emory looked down at himself and saw a bloody and bruised body. The young man tapped his own temple, and Emory examined his. He discovered a four-inch gash and felt sticky, gritty blood on the side of his face.

"There was… a wreck."

The young man pulled a handkerchief from his pocket, then opened his bottle of water and wetted the cloth. He handed it to Emory and looked toward the tunnel.

"A wreck? Anyone else hurt?"

Emory nodded as he used the handkerchief to wipe his face clean, then his forearms and hands.

The man looked into the tunnel. As he did, Emory noticed a silver bicycle laying on the sidewalk.

"Is that your bike?" Emory asked.

The man kept his eyes on the tunnel and strolled toward it. "Nope. Was here when I got here." He paused. "Hey, is anyone else hurt?"

Emory moved to the bike and stood it up. "They're dead," he said as he swung his leg over the bike and sat down.

His bony knees barely cleared the space between the pedals and handlebars, but it would have to do. He hadn't ridden a bicycle since, well, he couldn't even recall. He hoped it was true that you never forgot how to do it.

The young man turned back at Emory. "Who's dead?"

Emory pointed the bicycle toward the city and glanced over his shoulder at the man.

"Everyone."

He pushed on the pedals. The bike wobbled at first, and he thought he might crash into the railing, but soon enough, it steadied out. He peddled faster and didn't look back.

CHAPTER TWENTY-THREE

MINA STAYED in the hallway while the nurses and doctor rushed into the room and conversed in their alien medical jargon. The commotion lasted about five minutes, and when they fell silent, Mina knew what was up. She'd had plenty of experience with bad news in her life, and it got to be that you could see it coming.

The doctor, a Middle-Eastern man with shoe-leather brown skin, stepped out of the room first. He rested his palm on Mina's shoulder. "I'm very sorry. We did all we could," he said.

Mina nodded. "It's all right."

He moved on with a brief, consoling smile. The nurses shuffled out in a row after him, reminding Mina of ants. The last nurse in line paused.

"You can go in with him now," the nurse said.

"Do I have to?"

"Excuse me?"

Mina shook her head. "Nothing. Sorry."

The nurse looked at her quizzically before following her co-workers down the hospital hallway.

Mina hesitated, then re-entered the room. Sprawled on the bed was the body of her dead father, a blue sheet pulled up to just under his chin.

She reclaimed her seat beside the bed and wondered what happened next. Were there papers that needed signing? Was she supposed to call a funeral home? She needed an instructional pamphlet or maybe a book. *What to Do After Your Daddy Dies for Dummies.*

Mina thought Google might provide some answers and took her cell phone from her pocket. Upon turning it on, she saw there was no signal, so she moved to the window to try there. She stared out onto the soulless, industrial city as she waited to see if the phone might decide to work.

With her back turned, she didn't see Vernon sit up in the bed. The sheet slid off him to reveal the wiry white hair that dotted his bony torso in random patches. As he swung his legs over the side of the bed, the sheet fell to the floor.

Vernon stood up, his tighty whities, which had long ago stopped being tight or white, stood out in stark contrast against his dark exposed skin. He meandered toward his daughter, who still stared down at her phone.

Reflected movement in the glass caught her attention. She assumed— hoped—it was someone coming to tell her they needed to take the body to the morgue and she could go home. When she turned and saw her dead father looking straight at her, surprise was an under- statement.

Vernon's gray eyes had lost the rage that filled them in life. A vacant yet desperate stare had replaced his hate. He took a step toward Mina, then reached for her. Mina stepped back and hit the window, her bony elbow made a tiny tinking noise against the glass.

"Daddy?"

Vernon's mouth fell open, but instead of words, he exhaled a ragged gasp, and drool spilled out of his mouth in thick opaque strings.

He reached again for Mina. This time, his clumsy hands caught the neckline of her blouse. His fingers clawed at the fabric and the top button popped off. Mina swatted at his hand, and he growled at her and tried to drag her to him.

The other buttons gave way, and her shirt fell open to reveal her practical, largely unnecessary, white bra. Mina's initial surprise faded, and she pushed him away. Vernon stumbled back two steps but recovered and moved toward her again. He fell against her this time, his flesh pressed against hers, and he tried to bite her face, but Mina tilted her head back as far as possible and avoided his snapping jaws.

Mina kicked out, and her knee connected with his groin. He didn't go down like she'd hoped he would, but the momentary distraction allowed her to spin away and dash past him. Vernon turned, his movements slow and jerky, and came for her again.

Mina knew there was enough space that she could run past him and briefly considered it. But she was sick of running. Instead, she grabbed the metal bed pan from the small, particle board nightstand beside the bed and waited until he was close enough.

Vernon took three more lumbering steps in Mina's direction, and when he was within arm's length, she swung the bedpan with every bit of force her tiny body could summon.

The metal slammed into the side of Vernon's head with a hollow *thud*. She reared back and swung again. That blow sent him to his knees and split the top of his head open. Blood ran down his face in red rivulets. His mouth gaped open and shut, open and shut, and he reminded Mina of a fish gasping for air.

Mina stood before him and raised the bedpan over her head. She swung it one last time, heard a crunch as it hit, and Vernon collapsed to the floor motionless.

Mina dropped the bedpan, and the sound as it banged against the tile made her jump. She realized she was shaking all over and sat on the edge of the bed to steady herself. She looked down at her twice-dead father.

I should have done that a long time ago, she thought.

CHAPTER TWENTY-FOUR

IT WAS over ninety degrees in the bus, and Bundy had worked up a bad case of swamp ass. He sat near the back, taking up one of the green vinyl seats all by himself. Allebach had the seat across the aisle from him.

Bundy had grown fond of Allebach during his short stay at the prison. He reminded him a lot of the fellows Bundy would meet at the shooting range or butcher shops. Allebach was what Bundy's father would have called 'a good egg,' and the two men were in the middle of a deep conversation about nothing at all.

Bundy noticed Errickson glaring at them from the front of the bus. He kept his eyes on Allebach but tilted his head toward the younger guard.

"I don't believe he approves of you treating me like a genuine human being."

Allebach wasted no energy looking toward his colleague. "Kids come into the system thinking it's their job to punish people. That isn't what we're here for. You're already doing your time. We're supposed to make that go as smooth as possible. Nothing more, nothing less."

Bundy grinned. "Might want to tell him that."

"Some of them wise up. Ones that don't, well, they end up as bitter and angry as the men they spent their whole careers hating."

The bus had been moving in slow motion for the last half hour, but Bundy noticed that it picked up pace as it rolled into a tunnel. The warm light of day disappeared in an instant, plunging the bus into darkness.

"What's going on?" one of the sick prisoners asked. "Where are we?" His voice was slow and delirious.

Bundy heard the sound of shackles clanging against metal. That was followed by coughing, then more movement.

"Back in your fucking seats!" Errickson yelled, and Bundy could hear the fear he was trying to cover with rage.

The putrid green light of dim fluorescents chased away most of the darkness and revealed two of the sick prisoners up and moving. It also showed Errickson was holding a small pistol.

"Sit down, now!"

Bundy watched the reckless little asshole sweep the gun back and forth, his finger on the trigger and one panicked moment away from pulling it and shooting God knows what or who.

"Put that away, Errickson!" Allebach ordered, but the kid kept waving it around like he was ready to waste the entire bus.

The bus driver also watched the chaos unfolding behind him, ignoring the road ahead. Bundy, much to his dismay, did catch what was happening through the windshield.

"Boss, you better tell that driver to stop."

"What?" Allebach asked, but it was already too late.

———

Bundy never lost consciousness, but his bell was ringing by the time the momentum of the crash had ceased. He ended up wedged between two vinyl seats.

The bus itself had toppled onto the passenger side. Noxious smoke rolled in through the broken windows. Bundy gagged and coughed as it burned his nasal passages. Then he realized, for the first time since they left the prison, no one else was coughing.

Bundy grabbed the edges of the seats that had him pinned and pulled himself up. It took all his strength, and the exertion, coupled with the effects of the crash, made his head spin. Fortunately, the copious amount of sweat that covered his body acted as a lubricant, and he managed to squeeze free.

None of his fellow passengers were moving. Two of the prisoners laid limp over seats, but everyone else was unseen. With the bus on its side, Bundy had to crawl over the windows to move. He felt the broken glass dig into his knees and shins, but pushed aside the pain. He needed to find Allebach.

Bundy found him four rows up. The man was head down, ass up, and motionless. Bundy gave his legs a shove, and he somersaulted backward. His head slumped sideways atop a swollen, purple neck. Bundy knew that was game over. He grabbed the chain around Allebach's waist and retrieved the keys for his cuffs.

As Bundy freed himself from the manacles, he looked down at the man and felt his chest tighten. Allebach was indeed a good egg, one who reminded Bundy of his own dad, who'd died of heart failure a decade ago. They even had the same wispy, gray combover.

"Shitty way to go out, Boss. You deserved better."

Bundy didn't realize he was crying until he felt a tear run down his nose and tickle his nostril. He rolled the old guard into a laying down position and folded his hands over his belly. Next, he wiped the glass off the man's face. He then set to fixing Allebach's hair, but as he tried to get it right, the dead man opened his eyes.

Bundy fell backwards and cracked his already foggy head against the metal interior.

"Boss?"

Allebach sat up, and when Bundy leaned toward him, the guard swatted at him and caught the upper part of his ear.

Bundy felt the cartilage bend and flesh tear. How could the old guy be so damned strong? Bundy swung out with his meaty right arm and connected with Allebach's face. He tumbled backward again, and Bundy got on his knees.

He saw the old guard get up again, unfazed by the blow, and then he noticed more movement out of the corner of his eye.

The two prisoners he'd seen strewn over the seats were now up and moving. Past them, another prisoner was chewing on a severed head that Bundy recognized as belonging to Cob. No more corn for you, amigo.

Zombies. They're zombies. He never believed in that kind of thing, but unless he'd hit his head hard enough to scatter all his marbles, there was no other way around it.

As the realization settled in, he felt Allebach grab his leg. Bundy kicked back with his size fourteen foot and smashed it into his mouth. He heard teeth snap like dry wood.

With most of the zombies ahead, fleeing via the front was a no-go. Bundy turned back and crawled toward the emergency exit. Along the way, he found Errickson's pistol. It was a tiny .22 Magnum pocket revolver, which was woefully inaccurate unless you wanted to shoot someone in the gut from two feet away.

It looked and felt like a cap gun in Bundy's monstrous hand. Little prick probably thought it was an Al Capone gangster gun. Bet he paid twice what it was worth, too. He must have kept it in an ankle holster so he could smuggle it into the prison even though doing so was a felony. Talk about the inmates running the asylum.

Still, it was better than nothing, so Bundy took it as he crawled toward the door at the rear of the bus. When he got there, he half expected it to be jammed, but when he pulled the latch release, it flopped out and open, where it hit the exterior of the bus with a bang that echoed through the confines of the tunnel.

Bundy threw one leg through the door, then the other as he managed his girth through the opening. He barely fit when it was right side up, let alone sideways. He dropped down to the pavement and felt the impact of his five hundred pounds in all his joints when he landed.

All he could see ahead of the bus was smoke, crashed vehicles, and zombies. Behind it, the smoke was less dense, the totaled cars fewer. Only a few zombies, all of them preoccupied with eating the victims of the crash, were behind him. He went with that option.

A hundred yards away, a vintage Firebird sat pinned nose to nose with a Lincoln Navigator, and together they blocked his escape route. As Bundy hauled himself onto the hood of the Pontiac, a hand grabbed the waistband of his standard-issue orange jumpsuit.

He turned, looked over his shoulder, and saw Errickson. His glasses sat askew on his face. One lens had shattered, and a large sliver punctured his eyeball. The remaining eye was lifeless and blank but somehow still seeing, and when Bundy's face fell into view, the short man gasped and screwed up his face like a fellow who'd just smelled a particularly sour fart.

"Still an asshole, even when you're dead," Bundy said.

Bundy reached back and tried to grab the man's hair, but it was slick with blood and too short for him to get a grip. Errickson's head darted forward, and Bundy pulled back his hand just in time to avoid losing a finger or two.

Beyond them, Bundy could see more of the undead drifting through the haze toward them. Errickson lunged at him again, but, this time, Bundy struck back with his oversized hand and punched him in his good eye.

The force of the blow sent the guard to his knees, and Bundy used that opportunity to extract the gun from his pocket. As Errickson struggled back to his feet, Bundy aimed the small barrel of the Magnum at his face.

"Wish I could say I'm sorry about this, but."

He pulled the trigger, and the .22 punched a hole in the space just below the dead guard's nose. His teeth folded inward in a spray of blood and white shrapnel. The bullet didn't have enough force to vacate his skull, but it got the job done just as well, and Errickson tumbled to the pavement.

By this time, the approaching zombies were close enough that Bundy could make out their physical features. That was too close, and he climbed over the hood of a Pontiac. As he did, he spotted two bloody toddlers clawing at the windows of the crashed Lincoln. They fought to get out, or get to him. Either way, he ignored them. He wasn't fond of children, especially undead ones.

Past that obstacle, he had a somewhat clear path. He ran or, more accurately, strolled briskly away from the crashed vehicles, keeping a good distance between himself and the occasional zombies he passed along the way. They ignored him, too, busy feasting on other casualties or the pileup.

As he came toward the tail end of the pileup, he found a VW Beetle with the driver's door ajar and the engine still running. A few yards away, a zombie in a pinstripe suit was eating the shapely thigh of a girl who looked about college age. Bundy imagined that the Bug was hers and that she'd had the bad luck of being a Good Samaritan at the wrong time.

Her loss was his gain, though, and he pushed the seat back as far as it would go and squeezed himself into the car. He turned it around in the tunnel and weaved his way through the remaining vehicles until he reached daylight.

Dozens of cars inbound for the tunnel had stopped at the entrance. The smoke that drifted out of the tube must have given them second thoughts about entering. Bundy steered by them, aiming the Bug toward the outbound lanes. The metal underbelly of the car scraped as he crested the concrete median.

A middle-aged man in a Honda yelled out to him. "Hey, buddy! What happened in there?"

Bundy looked at the driver and his wife, then glanced back toward the tunnel. "Take my advice and head for the hills."

"Should we call the cops?"

"The cops? You better call the damned Marines."

The man gawked at him, confused.

"Is that man a convict?" the wife asked.

Bundy floored it, continued over the median, and bounced down into the outbound lane. Why, yes, Ma'am, I'm Inmate 2089349. Pleased to meet you. Yinz have a good day. Oh, and watch out for the zombies.

CHAPTER TWENTY-FIVE

EVERYTHING WAS GOING AS WELL as possible under the circumstances until the slob in the Dykstra jersey fell. While running north, the group had put fifty yards between themselves and the zombie horde, thanks to zigzagging through alleyways and between buildings. It was almost 11 a.m., and they had no real destination aside from getting as far as possible from the city before the bombs rained down.

Peduto saw the Smart Car first. The tiny, black and white convertible looked like a toy, but it sat undamaged in the middle of the road and the driver was nowhere to be seen. She jumped inside and found the key in the ignition. One turn and it fired right up.

"Get in!" she called. The ridiculousness of the order was obvious, and she knew that. The car had no rear seat and room for only two up front.

"Peduto, drive. Bolivar, you get in the passenger seat. Me and him will hold on," Sawyer said, jerking a thumb at Dykstra Jersey.

"No, I'll ride on the outside," Bolivar said, but Sawyer's *Shut up and do what I tell you to do*' look settled that matter, and he climbed in beside Gwen.

The top was down, and Sawyer grabbed hold of the roll bar in the back.

"Giddy up," he said to Dykstra Jersey, and the man wrapped his forearms around the bar. "Now roll!"

Peduto did. The car was slow under normal circumstances, and, with four people on board, it felt like the engine was powered by a hamster wheel. It was still quicker than the zombies.

They made it a few miles before Dykstra Jersey's grip became weak, and he almost fell.

Sawyer saw his distress. "Don't you let go."

The man nodded but couldn't mask the pain in his face.

When they rounded a corner, a group of more than forty zombies blocked their path. Peduto hit the brakes, and that's when the man lost his grip. Sawyer reached out with his right arm and caught him by the sleeve of his jersey, but the man was beyond his tipping point and there was no pulling him back.

As he fell, Sawyer went down too, and his M4 slammed to the pavement underneath him. Dykstra Jersey shrieked. It was the high-pitched sound of a wounded animal. Peduto had stopped the car, and when Bolivar looked back, he saw the Phillies fan's leg was twisted outward at an angle human legs aren't meant to bend.

Sawyer hopped up and ran to him. He lifted the man, who screamed again, and his broken leg swayed back and forth like a metronome.

The zombies marched toward them from the front and closed the gap to a few yards. Peduto threw open her door and got one step out before Sawyer screamed at her.

"Get back in that car!"

She paused, and Sawyer's face flamed red. "That's an order, Corporal!"

Peduto pulled her leg back into the car and closed the door.

"God, Jesus! Put me down!" Dykstra Jersey wailed.

"What do I do?" Peduto shouted to Sawyer, Bolivar, and herself.

Through the windshield, Bolivar could see the closest zombie was less than twenty feet away. The others weren't far behind.

Sawyer saw them, too. "Oh, fuck it all to hell."

He dropped Dykstra Jersey, who hit the ground with another anguished cry. Sawyer left him there and dashed to the Smart Car, only pausing a moment to look at Peduto.

"I'll clear the middle. You keep driving. Stay on Penrose until you find a ramp for 95 South." Peduto reached for his hand, and Sawyer jerked it away. "I don't know if there's going to be anyone left, but try for the Air Force base in Dover."

He looked to the zombies, which were now within what Bolivar's grandfather would have called spitting distance. "Go there. Or don't. I got a feeling it don't matter anymore."

With that, he rushed ahead of the car and opened fire on the crowd of zombies. To Bolivar, they looked like the metal ducks at carnival shooting booths as they fell under the fire of Sawyer's M4. All that was missing was the plinking sound.

As promised, Sawyer created a lane through the center of the horde large enough for the Smart Car, and Peduto floored it. As she steered the car through the mass of them, the zombies clawed and swiped at the vehicle. One caught Bolivar's cap and whisked it clean off.

The convertible clipped a few of them, pushing them aside like bumper cars. They snarled and growled and tried to regroup, but the car was almost through them. Just before they got to the end of the pack, a zombie in a suit jumped onto the hood.

It peered in through the glass, and Bolivar thought the man looked to have been in his thirties. Gel held his hair in a perfect pompadour. He looked almost normal, except for the dead, gray eyes and the bloody drool that seeped from his mouth.

The zombie grabbed hold of the top of the windshield and dragged himself up onto it. His face pressed against the glass and flattened all his features. He kept pulling himself upward. Another two feet and he'd be able to reach inside the convertible.

Before it could do that, Bolivar pulled out the pistol Peduto had given him a few hours earlier. He pressed it against the windshield. Only the quarter-inch pane of glass separated the barrel from the zombie's face.

"Do it," Peduto said.

Bolivar didn't wait. He squeezed the trigger, and spider webs burst across the windshield. A small hole appeared in the center of them as the bullet penetrated the glass, then slammed into the zombie's face. It tumbled off the car and rolled a few times when it hit the ground.

CHAPTER TWENTY-SIX

WIM STARED at Old Man Bender's undead family and pondered what to do. He felt like kicking himself for not bringing a second firearm and even more so for putting his life at risk over chocolate ice cream. He hoped there would be time for scolding himself later on. Right now, he needed to focus on surviving.

The tot that clung to his leg was also biting him and the only thing saving his flesh from the boy's sharp, little teeth was the denim of his blue jeans. Wim took the empty pistol and grabbed it by the barrel. He brought it down on the zombie's head as hard as he could. The boy dropped to his knees but wasn't dead.

That bought Wim a few seconds of time. He scanned the freezer, looking for anything he could use as a weapon. In the near dark, it was almost impossible to see. One of the fathers was only a few feet away and closing in fast. Wim grabbed the feet of the boy he'd knocked down and hoisted him into the air.

The boy weighed no more than forty pounds, far less than a bag of feed, and Wim had no trouble swinging him by his feet and using him like a club. The tot's head connected with the skull of the man, which resulted in a sharp crack and hollow thud, like knocking together two pieces of dead wood. Wim supposed that, in a way, that's all they were.

The adult zombie wobbled on his feet, took half a step forward, then two back, then collapsed. The boy had also gone limp, and Wim launched him at the others like he was throwing a shot put.

The pint-sized zombie crashed into the others, knocking down two of the children and pushing back the remaining adults. Wim ran a detour around them, and, as he did, he almost ran into one of the meat hooks hanging from the ceiling. That gave him an idea.

Wim snatched a hook from the line and gripped it by the wooden handle. He turned back to the zombies and saw the younger brother was within arm's reach. He swung the hook and the pointed end punched through the man's temple. The brother fell so quick that it pulled the hook loose from Wim's grip.

Wim jerked it free and saw one of the children blocking his path to the freezer door. In two long strides, he reached the girl and slammed the meat hook upward, catching her under the chin. It poked out through her eye socket, and her cloudy, blue orb popped free and then dangled from the gaping hole like a spent parachute.

She kept moving, so Wim gave the handle a hard yank and threw her across the room, where she crashed into a pile of boxes. Wim now had a clear path, and he took it.

He shoved his shopping cart through the opening, grabbed the door, and slammed it shut, knocking over one of the wife zombies in the process. He latched the door from the outside and leaned back against it as he caught his breath.

Wim couldn't believe how close he'd come to dying and was surprised at how much the prospect of death had frightened him. Maybe he had something to live for after all.

It was almost pitch black outside now, and he checked each direction multiple times, like a little boy crossing the street, as he exited the store. Much to his relief, the streets were still empty. He transferred his groceries from the cart to the Bronco, then reloaded his pistol, just in case.

Even though life was lonely on the farm with no one and nothing around, he couldn't wait to go back. He'd deal with everything else tomorrow. If there was a tomorrow. Any more, he couldn't be sure.

CHAPTER TWENTY-SEVEN

RAMEY LAID ON HER BACK, her eyes closed and earbuds blocking out the sounds of the dying world. She knew that once she left her bedroom, she might find her mother dead on the couch. Or maybe she'd be unconscious with puke all over herself, the furniture, and the floor. Or maybe she'd be high as hell, trying to make mac and cheese in the microwave, even though the electricity was out. She was in no rush to see which scenario was true.

She didn't hear the first soft thud at her bedroom door. Or the second. The third was louder. Loud enough to draw her attention through the white noise of her earbuds. She pulled out one of them and listened. Soon enough, a fourth came.

The next thud was louder and harder and followed by what sounded like a pencil breaking.

"Mom?"

Ramey removed the other earbud and dropped them on the bed. She stood and crossed the small room, but when she reached the door, she held the knob in her hand but didn't open it.

"Mom?" she asked again.

There came another thud. This time, Ramey thought she heard a soft moan. She turned the doorknob, and as soon as the latch cleared, the strike plate the door pushed inward. Ramey stumbled as the door knocked her backward, and she landed on her butt.

When she looked up, she saw Loretta shuffling into the room. Her nose was smashed to the side and laid flat against her cheek like a chunk of raw chicken. So that's what I heard snap, Ramey thought. A syringe hung from Loretta's arm, the needle still embedded in her skin, and a small trail of dried, brown blood traversed the leathery skin of her forearm.

She's dead.

No, that couldn't be true. Dead people don't walk around. This was just some terrible reaction to the drugs. That's what it had to be.

Loretta lunged, or more precisely, fell toward her with a gurgling growl. When Ramey rolled out of the way, Loretta face planted on the shag carpet without making the slightest attempt to catch herself.

Nope. Definitely dead.

Loretta clawed at Ramey's bare leg, and her fingernails scraped off the top layer of skin but didn't draw blood. Ramey reared back and kicked her mother in the face, her Sketchers connecting with Loretta's jaw and resulting in a crack that Ramey both heard and felt. Loretta's head snapped backward, then flopped forward again into the carpet.

Ramey ran past her mother, out of the bedroom, and to the kitchen. She jerked open the junk drawer and dug through the tools and bottle openers and hot pads and toothpicks as she searched for the keys to Loretta's car but came up empty.

"Shit!" Ramey said as she slammed the drawer closed. She checked the countertops, but there were no keys to be found.

Ramey looked up to see Loretta back on her feet and shambling into the living room. Her dislocated jaw jutted to the right, the opposite direction her nose faced, and Ramey had a second to think that her dead mother looked like something out of a Picasso painting.

Loretta was now between Ramey and the trailer door. Ramey returned to the junk drawer and looked for anything she could use. She shoved aside the pliers and cookie cutters and bolts and found something worthwhile: the meat tenderizer. She grabbed the rubber handle and turned back toward her mother.

"Get out of my way, Mom!"

Loretta kept shuffling at her, oblivious to her daughter's demands.

Ramey tried to go around her, but Loretta caught her shirt sleeve. She leaned into Ramey and tried to bite, but her jaw couldn't close, and she only drooled all over her.

Ramey swung the silver tenderizer, and it smashed into Loretta's forehead, leaving a waffle pattern in her dead flesh. Ramey swung again, this time bringing the tool down on the top of her head.

The skin split open to reveal gleaming, white bone underneath. Ramey hit her a third time, and the tool caught her in the temple, and Loretta crashed to the floor in an unmoving heap. Ramey jumped over her body and ran out of the trailer.

Outside, the park was in chaos. It seemed as if all of her neighbors were either chasing someone or being chased.

Ramey stood on the porch and watched the eight-year-old Sutton twins run down Mr. Reese, the retiree who lived three trailers down. They pounced on him as he fell and started eating him. He kept screaming until one of the twins chewed his throat out.

Joan Saylor, who sometimes cut Ramey's hair for free when she couldn't afford to go to the Walmart salon, sat in her front yard and munched on the arm of a man Ramey assumed to be Mr. Saylor. She couldn't tell because his face was gone.

Drea, a butch biker chick who was always tinkering with her vintage Harley Davidson trike, used her wrench to knock out the teeth of Louie Fritz, a creeper who Loretta fancied and once invited in for lunch, only he spent most of the time trying to look down Ramey's shirt or up her shorts instead of paying attention to Loretta.

Ramey rather enjoyed watching his teeth go flying through the air like a handful of chiclets, but as soon as he was incapacitated, another zombie grabbed Drea from behind and chomped into her shoulder. The biker was big, over six feet—Ramey had always suspected she was a man in drag—and she hurled the zombie over her broad shoulders and onto the gravel driveway.

Drea raised the wrench to hit Louie again, but before she could act, her body spasmed, and she collapsed to her knees. She dropped her weapon, and when the convulsions stopped, she stood back up and chased after a girl Ramey used to go to school with but who had dropped out after getting pregnant at fourteen.

Ramey stepped off the porch and rushed to Loretta's old Dodge. She opened the door as quietly as possible and dropped into the driver's seat, where she checked the ignition for keys that weren't there.

When Ramey looked back up, she saw Louie the Creeper looking through the windshield at her. His combover was pushed askew from his earlier tumble, and it stuck almost straight up in a thinning, gray mohawk.

Ramey scrambled out of the car and waited for him to make the first move. When he ran at her, she swung the meat tenderizer, and it hit the bridge of his nose with a pleasant crunch that reminded her of cracking open a fortune cookie.

Confucius say zombie no match for girl with hammer.

She could hear the sound of an engine running and sprinted around the trailer to the opposite lane, where a jacked-up pickup painted primer gray and with as much putty as metal idled in the middle of the road. The driver's side door hung ajar, but the cab was empty.

Ramey ran to it, passing by Adele Miller, the park's office manager, who lumbered along dragging a dog leash with no dog at the other end. Ramey jumped into the truck and pulled the door shut.

She threw the truck into gear, thankful that they were too poor for an automatic and she'd learned to drive a stick, and gunned the engine. As she did, a burly man with an American flag bandanna tied around his forehead and carrying a flat-screen TV ran out of the closest trailer.

"That's my truck!"

Ramey slammed the gas, and the almost bald tires squealed as the truck took off.

"You bitch, bring back my truck!"

Ramey checked the rear-view mirror and saw him toss down the TV. He chased her for a few paces but gave up as she gained ground.

She was almost at the exit when she saw Bobby Mack, the de-virginizer, stumble into her path. Bobby's white wife beater tank top was red with blood and his right arm looked like a half-eaten hamburger.

Ramey didn't slow down, and the chrome bumper hit Bobby at thirty miles an hour. He bounced a few feet into the air, allowing her one last look at his dim face before he crashed back down. She heard bones break as the truck rolled over him. She might have even smiled a little.

CHAPTER TWENTY-EIGHT

MEAD NEVER MADE it back to his apartment. As he drove away from the buffet, it became clear the world had turned to shit over the last few hours. He saw zombies in the streets, zombies trapped inside cars, and zombies eating humans.

The few live and uninjured people he saw were running for their lives. He saw no first responders or anyone interested in coming to the rescue, a fact that did not surprise him. There wasn't anyone in Johnstown worth saving, anyway.

As he drove, he passed a small sporting goods store, saw the plate-glass window shattered, and stopped. He crawled through the opening, careful to not impale himself on any of the larger shards, which clung to the frame like jagged teeth.

He kept his eyes forward as he dropped into the building, watching for both zombies and looters. He came down on a chunk of concrete, the source of the destroyed window, and went sprawling into the broken glass.

"Fuck!" He climbed to his knees and wiped bits of glass from his arms and legs. Aside from a few minor scrapes, he was fine. Be more careful, dumbass, he thought as he stood. His ankle was sore but not sprained.

A torn ligament or broken leg in a situation like this would be the end of him. He knew that. Mead wasn't stupid, even if most of his teachers and his parents would have said otherwise. He knew he could survive this.

He had always been a zombie fanatic, whether they were piece of shit Italian gore-fests by guys like Fulci, Lenzi, and Mattei or the more cerebral Romero movies. Mead watched them all, and, sadly, he now thought he always rooted for the zombies.

It wasn't that he hated everyone, although in real life, he loathed his fair share. No, in the movies, the heroes were always idiots. They deserved to die because they did stupid things like try to save babies or old people. Or they didn't look where they were going and stumbled right into the zombies. Or they holed up inside a building where they ended up surrounded and trapped. He'd be smart.

A large display case by the cash register was also smashed open and emptied. Mead had never been in that store in his life, but he could tell by the price tags that it had housed firearms once upon a time.

That was okay—he didn't want a gun. The closest he'd ever come to firing a pistol was playing Duck Hunt on his old school Nintendo, and, more often than not, he missed the ducks, and the damned dog laughed at him. Besides, guns jammed. Or you ran out of bullets and had to go hunting for more ammo. He wouldn't fall into that trap. That was just another easy way to die.

Mead examined the store and found it empty of anything currently or formerly human. As he searched, he grabbed a few buck knives, but he wanted something he could use without getting so up close and personal. He sorted through a rack of wooden and aluminum baseball bats. He considered one, but they also seemed too short. The bows and arrows he came across next were even more useless to him than guns.

He'd almost given up hope and decided to make his stand with one of the bats when a rack of hockey sticks caught his eye. A sign above them read "The first truly unbreakable sticks" and beneath that, a price sign listed them as "Starting at only $149."

"Jesus. Who has that kind of money for a stick?" he said to himself. When he picked up one of the sticks, he was amazed at how light it was. Maybe a pound, if that. The shaft and blade were metal. It seemed impossible that something that felt so inconsequential in hand could be unbreakable. It must be some sort of modern-day alchemy.

To test this out, Mead stepped to the cash register, the drawer of which hung open and empty. Idiots, Mead thought. Money was worthless now.

He raised the stick above his head and swung down as hard as he could manage. The metal whistled through the air like a sword before crashing into the plastic machine. Mead felt electric shockwaves fire through his arms. The plastic frame of the cash register shattered into large chunks, but the hockey stick remained in one piece without so much as a dent.

"Well, holy shit!" Screw the Ark of the Covenant; Mead had just found something much more practical. The stick was five feet long, well beyond arm's reach and would be exactly what he needed with a little customization.

Mead scavenged the store. When he finished, he felt he was more than adequately suited for going to war against some zombie bastards. He taped large knives to the butt ends of two hockey sticks, then followed that up with taping two ice skate blades around the blade of the stick. He checked their sharpness by lightly touching the blade against his forearm and opened an inch-long gash. Perfect.

He used heavy-duty backpack straps to fasten the double-bladed hockey sticks crisscrossed over his back. He wrapped his arms and legs in duct tape, only allowing enough empty space for his joints to bend.

He found a lacrosse helmet that even had a cage to protect his face. He slid a variety of knives into a utility belt, then finished off the outfit with a pair of heavy-duty steel-toed boots and thick leather gloves. He'd gained about thirty pounds' worth of armor but had a feeling it would be more than worth its weight.

Mead crawled back out the window and hopped down to the street. A dilapidated duplex further up the block was ablaze, and orange-yellow flames clawed out open windows. A woman, half her skin charred black, wandered down the street. An elderly man, so stooped over he looked like a hunchback, loped toward her.

"Oh, God, miss! We need to get you help!" the man said.

What a fool, Mead thought. When the old fart grabbed hold of the burned woman's uninjured side, and she responded by jumping on him and tearing open his throat, his skepticism was proved correct. The geezer didn't even have time to scream.

Mead ignored them both and retreated to his Cavalier. He deposited one of the hockey sticks in the back seat and went to follow up with the second but paused. Mead glanced back at the burned zombie who had moved on from the geezer's neck and was now dining on his face like it was an Easter ham.

He moved up the sidewalk, walking at first, then changing gears to a quick jog as he got closer. He was in a full sprint by the time he reached them.

"Head's up, bitch!"

She looked up, a ragged piece of flesh dangling from her mouth. Mead swung the end of the hockey stick with the skate blade attached.

The blade hit her in the temple and tore through the front of her face, slicing through her right eye, the bridge of her nose, then the left eye before ripping free at the opposite end of her head. She tumbled backward and remained motionless on the sidewalk.

Who needs Sidney Crosby? Mead thought, and he fought hard to suppress a primal scream of victory. Got to be careful. You don't know how many zombies are out there.

The hunchback on the ground had stopped bleeding, and when Mead looked down at him, he saw his dead eyes open. The lifeless thing tried to growl, but with most of the bottom half of its face missing, it came out in more of a gurgle. It reached up, swatting at Mead but only caught air.

Mead straddled the zombie and spun the hockey stick around (like a ninja, he thought with glee). Now, the knife's end faced downward. He clenched the shaft with both hands and guided the knife into the zombie's eye.

He stopped pushing when he felt resistance from hitting the back of the monster's skull. Mead gave the stick a quick jerk from side to side to make sure the creature's brains were scrambled. The zombie went limp.

Mead stepped off it and jogged back to his car. He set the now bloody stick in the passenger seat for easy access. The Cavalier started with a loud backfire, and as Mead drove away, several zombies, drawn to the sound, followed.

CHAPTER TWENTY-NINE

THE RELIEF OFFICER NEVER ARRIVED, and three days later, Aben was still handcuffed to the toilet. He gave up and drank from the bowl halfway through day two. Even for a man who had slept in gutters and eaten from restaurant dumpsters, he felt that was a new low point.

Dolan's decomposing body laid where it fell in the center of the room. The smell of his rotting corpse filled the hot, cramped office. His exposed belly had swelled to three times its normal size, and Aben half expected it to burst like an overfilled water balloon.

The officer's skin had first gone pale white and more recently turned a putrid gray-green. His eyes bulged like they would pop from their sockets, and his black tongue jutted from his mouth like he was giving an undead raspberry.

Watching the decomposition process up close and personal was a fascinating, if revolting, way to pass the time, but what really bothered Aben were the flies. Thousands of them.

They invaded the room about ten minutes after Dolan died, like they had some sort of death sonar. Maybe they did. They landed on the body and the splattered blood and brains to eat and lay their eggs.

The next day, he saw the first maggots. He tried to tell himself his eyes were playing tricks on him. That it was hunger and dehydration, and he wasn't seeing what he thought he was. But toward the afternoon, they were large enough he couldn't deny it any longer.

The tiny, writhing worms crawled over the body, eating and burrowing into the dead flesh. He could see Dolan's skin pulsing and rippling as the worms ate him from the inside out.

Forget ashes to ashes, dust to dust. This is what happens when you die; you get eaten up and shit out by maggots, then more flies show up to eat their shit and lay more eggs, and round and round she goes. This is the circle of life. Hakuna matata.

Aben tried off and on to slip the cuff, but all he ended up with was a bloody and sore wrist. He'd seen prisoners break their thumbs to get out of handcuffs in the movies, but his were squeezed on so tight he doubted that would do any good.

Sooner or later, someone had to show up, and when they did, at least he'd have ten working fingers. There were two in particular he looked forward to showing them.

One thing he was not was hungry, and that surprised him as the last thing he'd eaten was the shitty pizza. Of course, it was hard to work up much of an appetite with a festering corpse twelve feet away.

Aben had almost resigned himself to the fact that the third day would come and go with no relief when he heard a thud and footsteps outside the office.

"Get in here! Officer Dolan shot himself!" Aben waited. The footsteps came closer but slow, so damn slow. Why the hell were they taking their time?

"Hey! Hurry up!"

The same plodding steps followed his plea.

Aben banged his handcuff chain against the pipe, which didn't do anything to speed up the footsteps and only made his raw wrist sore all over again.

Finally, a shape appeared near the doorway, but the hall outside the office was dark, and Aben couldn't make out any features.

"What the fuck are you waiting for?"

The figure stepped into the room, and Aben saw that the man who had just strolled into the office was only marginally better off than the dead policeman on the floor.

The man wore blue mechanic's overalls with a tag that read, "My name's Steve. What's yours?" but Steve didn't look like he was interested in small talk.

His flesh was lifeless and gray, and he had matching eyes. Dried blood covered the lower part of his face, and Aben swore he saw a hunk of skin—skin with human hair still attached to it—stuck between Steve's buck teeth.

She came back. That's what Dolan had said about his wife. She died but came back. Was that actually true? How the hell could that be?

Steve staggered into the room, his arms dangling limply at his sides. He saw Dolan's body on the floor, walked to it, and crumpled to his knees. He leaned over Dolan's lifeless corpse, grabbed an arm, and started eating.

Son of a bitch, he was right. Steve's a zombie, and now he's in here eating this rotten bastard right in front of me.

Now, the broken thumb trick sounded not only plausible but damned appealing. Aben grabbed the thumb on his cuffed left hand and tried squeezing it inward. He could feel the tendon stretch, and the knuckle gave a resounding pop, which sounded like a corkscrew blowing out of a champagne bottle in the small, quiet room.

Zombie Steve looked up at the sound of the knuckle cracking and he lost interest in the dead flesh before him. He rose to his feet and started toward fresh meat.

Aben's thumb hadn't broken, and, as Steve got closer, he tried again. He gritted his teeth and jerked his thumb outward, and the finger cracked again, but this time it was the joint separating. Hot pain shot up Aben's arm, and he pushed the dislocated thumb into his palm and pulled like hell against the cuffs.

His hand still refused to come free. He jerked hard, and the metal cuffs sliced further into his wrist. He could see the flesh gaping and blood running steadily from the red bracelet he'd carved.

The zombie took another step, but his foot came down on a chunk of Dolan's maggot-infested brains, and Steve's leg shot out from under him.

Aben watched the zombie pratfall with a mixture of amazement and horror. Steve flailed sideways, but his slow, awkward movements gave him no chance at stopping the plunge. The zombie fell through the air and landed on Dolan's distended midsection.

When the zombie fell on it, the skin covering Dolan's guts exploded. Aben had earlier thought of it like a water balloon, but when it burst, it became the most vile, revolting piñata in the history of the world.

Rotting intestines and tissue and black coagulated blood and maggots —my God, so many maggots—blew out like gory shrapnel. Aben only had a moment to take in the visual carnage before the smell hit him.

The aroma of the rotting corpse was fresh apple pie compared to the abomination that came from Dolan's insides. Aben gagged and retched, but after three days, he had no food to come up.

Another wave of the stench hit him. This time, when he gagged, yellow bile rocketed up his throat and burst out his mouth and nose. The bile ran down his chin and seeped through his beard, which only made him gag again.

His retching refocused the attention of Zombie Steve, who flailed atop Dolan's body like he was swimming in mid-air. His arms and legs smacked into the piles of rotten organs and maggots.

Steve grabbed a handful of something black and full of worms and shoved it into his mouth. After he swallowed it down, the zombie escaped his sandbar and was back on the hunt.

Aben pulled again and again, but his hand would not come free. He saw the top of his wrist was cut to the bone. Blood didn't simply run from the wound; it gushed.

The zombie was closing in, and Aben could see that his observation about the skin stuck on Steve's mouth was indeed correct. Apparently, Steve had recently dined on flesh a la blonde.

Aben could feel the zombie's rancid breath on his face. He knew he was about to die but decided to give it one more try.

Aben threw himself sideways with as much force as possible so that all of his body weight would be acting against the cuffs. He expected to end up hanging from them like a side of beef on a hook, dangling there for the zombie to feast upon, but to his amazement, he fell the whole way to the floor.

He was free.

Despite being loosed from the cuffs, Steve was almost on top of him. Aben belly crawled through the gore that had been Dolan's stomach, toward the cop's right hand, which still held his pistol. He could feel things squishing under his elbows and knees and didn't know whether they were intestines or maggots, and he didn't want to find out.

Aben pulled the gun free from the dead man's hand, rolled onto his back, and looked up at Zombie Steve.

"My name's Aben. And it definitely was not a pleasure meeting you."

Aben squeezed the trigger and shot Steve in the face. The zombie fell first to his knees, then forward, where he landed across Dolan's legs.

They all laid there for a moment, Aben and the two dead men. Then Aben looked at his left hand, which, only seconds earlier, had been cuffed.

What he saw first were the bones. He wasn't quite sure what he was seeing, and when he closed his hand, it was like looking at one of the skeletons in those Ray Harryhausen movies with stop motion animation. Only this was *his* hand.

The skin had been peeled away from his wrist all the way to his fingertips. He could see the tendons still attached to the white bone, but the flesh was gone. The pain was exquisite.

"Oh, shit," he said, and his head felt like it would float away. As fast as he could manage, he used his right hand to pull off his belt, then looped it around his left forearm and pulled it as tight as possible.

He was still holding on to the leather when he passed out.

CHAPTER THIRTY

THE MUSCLES in Emory's legs burned like they were aflame. He'd been peddling the bike for miles with intentions of going to the police station, but the further he rode into the city, the pointlessness of that plan became obvious. The horror he'd seen up close and personal inside the tunnel was not an isolated incident.

The first zombies he saw out here, in the light of day, were lone monsters staggering hither and yon like children lost in a foreign world. They wandered down the streets and sidewalks, bouncing off lampposts or street signs, then turned around to return in the direction from which they'd come. The ghouls would give a weak swipe as he rode by them but gave no chase.

They changed when he got further into the city, where the population was denser. Here, the zombies also increased in number, and rather than the lone wolves he saw on the outskirts, these zombies hunted in packs.

Emory was closing in on a discount electronics outlet when he saw three men with bandannas covering the lower halves of their faces rush toward the store. One of them carried a cinder block, which he hoisted over his head and pitched through the huge plate-glass window. It exploded in a thunderclap, and the trio jumped through the void.

Two of them reemerged moments later. The first carried an armload of laptops and tablets. The second had claimed a variety of cell phones. Their block tossing companion remained inside.

"Hurry up, Rog!" one of the thieves yelled.

A few seconds later, the other man hopped through the broken window carrying a flat-screen TV in each arm, and the men took off with their haul. They didn't make it to the end of the block before a group of eight zombies emerged from an alleyway and blocked their path.

Emory slowed the bike and considered another route, but his curiosity got the best of him, and he watched as the thief with the cell phones tossed them aside and pulled a pistol from the front of his jeans.

Without warning, the man fired four shots, and every round connected with the torso of a middle-aged zombie in a tank top. The four bullet holes stood out dramatically against the pale fabric and bits of blood seeped out. The zombie looked down at the holes in its chest and stomach, curious. Then, its gaze turned to the shooter.

"What the fuck?" the thief who held the flat screens said.

And then the zombies attacked like a pack of hyenas. They got the shooter first, and as he fell, he squeezed off another round that went whizzing down the street a few feet away from Emory.

The man screamed as the zombies ate him, taking ragged bites out of his arms, face, and neck. There were too many zombies to all get in on the meal, so the others moved on to the two remaining thieves.

The man who had the computers dropped them and abandoned his friends, sprinting in the opposite direction. He was fast, and within seconds, he was closing in on Emory. Up close, Emory could see this was no teenage thug. This man was in his forties, and old acne scars gave a lunar feel to his complexion.

"Can you believe this shit?" he asked Emory. "This is end of the world shit."

Emory watched the action ahead where the other thief now held up a TV like a shield, which he used to block and batter the zombies that were attacking him. One zombie got behind him and sunk its teeth into the man's shoulder.

He spun free and slammed the flat screen over the zombie's head. The plastic frame hung around the monster's throat like a necklace, but it didn't go down. Two more zombies grabbed the thief from behind, and soon enough, he was on the ground and being eaten alive.

"Hey! Gramps!" the last thief said to Emory, and the man's words drew his attention away from the carnage. He turned just in time to see a blurry fist flying at his face. He heard his nose break, and the momentum of the blow carried his slender frame backward. He tumbled off the bicycle and smacked into the pavement. Then the bike fell on top of him.

Through the stars that had sprung up before his eyes, he saw the man who had just assaulted him grab the bike and climb aboard. Emory reached out and grabbed the rear tire, but as the thief jumped down on the pedal, the spokes whirled around and spun free of his weak grip.

Gramps, Emory thought as he laid on the hard macadam and stared up at the featureless gray sky above him. Did that bastard have the audacity to call me Gramps?

As the stars faded and his senses returned, Emory realized the screaming had stopped. He rolled onto his side, then his knees, and as he knelt there on all fours like a dog in the street, he saw the zombies had finished dining on the electronics thieves and were coming for him.

His body still ached from the wreck, and his legs were weak from riding the bike. Getting to his feet seemed as impossible as climbing Mount Everest, an adventure he'd often daydreamed about tackling when he was a young man reading Sir Edmund Hillary's biography. But, like so many things, it had remained nothing more than a dream, one more unchecked box on his wish list of life.

Now, the only wish he had left was escaping the creatures which he could hear getting nearer, their lifeless feet scraping along the rough pavement.

He got one foot under him and used all his strength to stand. When he did, the stars returned, but now they were black pocks against the streetscape. A shrill bell went off inside his head, and it squealed so loud that he couldn't hear the zombies anymore.

A vise embraced his chest, and he struggled to suck in breath. He knew he was on the verge of losing consciousness and tried to blink away the coming darkness as his knees gave way.

That was when they grabbed him.

CHAPTER THIRTY-ONE

THE WOMAN CROUCHED on all fours and knelt over something, her head thrashing wildly back and forth. Solomon recognized her as one of the bints he'd heard gossiping about his wife. God rest her whoring soul. As he stepped closer, he saw exactly what was going on: she was chowing down on her own son. She had her head buried in the child's stomach, her face obscured in the tot's guts.

It reminded Solomon of a rabbit he'd had growing up. Daphne. She had gotten pregnant, and he'd waited impatiently as her furry belly grew fatter, eager to see the coming kits. She went into early labor one morning, and his mum allowed him to miss school so he could stay home for the event.

Daphne gave birth to five of the ugliest things he'd ever seen, but the experience amazed him nonetheless. He was even more amazed late that night when he poked his head into the hutch and saw mum rabbit eating her young.

Daphne's tan fur was stained red with blood. Two of the kits were back in her belly, albeit in a wholly different way than they'd been the day prior. She'd devoured a third from the hindquarters up, and its lifeless torso shimmied back and forth as its own mother dined on its organs.

An eight-year-old Solomon puked his supper onto his shoes and ran back into the house, crying as he told his mother of the horror. She looked at him blankly and only replied, "It happens, love. Part of nature."

After that, he had frequent nightmares in which his mum was eating him. He'd wake up in a cold sweat, crying and squalling, and she'd rush into the room to console him, but with those visions so fresh in his mind, he couldn't stand to look at her.

He pushed the thoughts of the rabbit and his mother from his mind and returned his focus to the zombie on the lawn before him. She was oblivious to his presence as he strolled up to her, held the pistol a few inches from the back of her skull and squeezed the trigger. Her head snapped forward, and she fell on top of the tot.

Solomon used his foot to push her off the lad, and when she toppled away, he saw the boy's stomach was a gaping cavern filled with half-eaten organs and ropes of chewed-on intestines. The aroma was nauseating, and Solomon used his free hand to cover his mouth and try to block out the stench.

The tot squirmed to and fro on its back, a whiny squeal coming from its mouth. Solomon wasn't sure if it was alive or undead, but what he needed to do was the same either way. He aimed the gun at the tiny body below him and—

"Put down the gun!"

He glanced to his side and saw two police officers standing in front of a police cruiser.

That's about right. Always get here after the fact. Solomon turned toward them. "Don't you coppers know what's going on here?"

The half-eaten tot rolled onto his stomach, and Solomon heard the guts slithering out of the gash in his belly as it moved toward him. Solomon moved his hand, the hand that held the gun, an inch, if that.

"Drop it, now!"

Solomon looked toward the cops, fury clouding his face. How stupid could these arses be?

He felt the tot's little hand press against his foot and looked down on it. He raised the pistol.

"No!"

When the cop screamed, Solomon turned his head toward the voice. The next thing he felt was a firecracker of pain explode in his head. Then everything went black.

———

I'M MOVING. MY BODY ISN'T, BUT I AM.

He couldn't see anything. Couldn't feel anything except an inferno in his head. He tried to move but couldn't. But he was moving.

"Get him in the ambulance!"

"Fuck him. He can rot."

"Jesus, Shawn, the guy got shot in the head."

"He's a fucking murderer. You see what he did to that woman and her kid?"

Between their voices came a metallic clang and a heavy bump that shook his body. Solomon realized he was on a stretcher. He tried to move again. Couldn't. Tied down to a stretcher. Balls did his head ache.

"We don't know what happened. Guy had a gun, and that kid... That didn't happen with a gun."

"I ain't no detective, but you got a bloody guy standing over a dead woman and a half-dead kid, and I know a duck when I see one."

Christ, these morons are my saviors?

The movement stopped. He heard a metal door opening. Felt the gurney bump against what he assumed was the ambulance, but he still couldn't see anything but black.

"What the?"

Someone screamed. A gunshot. Another.

"Hurry!"

He and the stretcher were thrown into the ambulance. He heard no one follow him into the back. Another door closed, and the tires squealed as the vehicle sped away. The stretcher bounced back and forth as the ambulance rounded corners at wildly unsafe speeds.

Muffled voices — Angry? Scared? — came from the front, but between the pain in his head and the shrieking of the siren, he couldn't make out any words. Soon enough, he lost consciousness anyway.

———

LIGHT SEEPED IN THROUGH THE DARKNESS. NOT MUCH BUT ENOUGH TO turn his world from a black hole into a dark room. A chorus of voices, some male, some female, shared this space with him.

"Where's Micklson?"

"He was supposed to be in the OR when we got here."

"Page him, now!"

"Yes, Doctor."

"Jesus, look at that hole. Is that his brain leaking out?"

"Where the fuck is Micklson? I'm not a god damned neurosurgeon."

A muffled scream rang out. Then another. Then several more.

"What now?"

"See what's going on out there. And tell someone to fucking get Micklson!"

A door opened, closed.

Solomon tried to open his eyes, and a flat plane of white appeared. Dark blobs moved through it. He made an attempt at speaking, but nothing came out.

More screams. His thoughts were cloudy and scattered, but he had an idea of what was happening, even if these fools were clueless. He forgot about trying to speak and focused on opening his eyes the rest of the way.

Something crashed. Glass broke.

His eyes came open, and he saw he was in an operating suite. Five other people stood around. He might as well have been invisible for all the attention they paid him. They stared at the double doors at the edge of the room. Doors that were at the very edge of his peripheral vision.

Yet another scream, this one high-pitched and filled with pain.

"Christ…"

All of them watched the doors, transfixed. Solomon saw a middle-aged man in dark blue scrubs grab a scalpel.

I'd go for something larger, Doc.

The doors burst open, and a woman in Winnie the Pooh scrubs fell through them. Doused in blood, she had a ragged hole where her right cheek had once resided. She ran into a wheeled table, knocking a tray of instruments to the floor where they clattered and scattered.

A woman and a man rushed to her side, kneeling out of Solomon's view. He saw a jowly cop stagger through the doors, the bottom half of his face covered in blood. Not his own blood.

Solomon tried to move and still couldn't. All he could do was lay there and watch as the cop grabbed an anesthesiologist by the front of her uniform and pulled her into him. He was much taller than her, and when he bit down, his teeth caught beneath her eye and above her eyebrow. There was a grating, scraping sound as his jaws closed.

The woman squealed and flailed at the cop with her fists. One of the nurses slammed a metal clipboard over the cop's head, stealing his attention. When he pulled back to look at his assailant, the anesthetist's eye dangled from his mouth.

The room became chaos. Running and fighting and crying and screaming and bleeding. So much bleeding. Solomon saw a slender, dark-haired man with jet black hair come through the doors. He was missing his nose and upper lip. That didn't stop him from tearing out the throat of one of the surgical techs. In the struggle, Solomon saw a blood-speckled name tag and was positive it read, "Micklson."

Well, that's fookin' fantastic.

He suspected there was no need to see what came next and let his eyes go shut.

CHAPTER THIRTY-TWO

MINA SAT on the bed for a good, long while and waited. She was certain that the police would show up any minute now. Killing her father had caused a heck of a racket, and some nurse or orderly must have called the cops to report the crazy black woman who had just committed patricide.

And when they showed up, what was she going to say? The truth? That her dead father came back to life and tried to kill her, only she bashed in his skull with the bedpan before he could eat her hardly seemed plausible. She was free of her father, only to end up in prison or, at best, a lunatic asylum. Either way, it would be bye, bye Birdie.

Only, no one showed up. No police. No security guards. Not even a nosy candy striper or janitor. She realized that all she had to do was walk away, and after cinching together her ripped blouse and trying her best to look like someone who hadn't just committed murder; she did just that.

Mina peeked out of the doorway and checked up and down the long corridor. All was clear, but not in the way she'd hoped. It wasn't that everyone was preoccupied. Everyone was gone.

Earlier, when she'd waited outside the room for the doctor and nurses to attempt their best heroic measures, the hall was bustling with hospital employees fluttering about like worker bees. Now, there was no one, as if everyone in the hospital had gone on a cigarette break at the exact same time.

Who cares where they all went, Mina thought. Just go. So, she did. She was halfway to the elevator when she heard someone moaning a few rooms down. As she got closer, she heard the steady tone of a hospital machine. Mina didn't know what the machine was or its purpose, but she knew from the movies the sound was bad news.

She again checked the hallway, but no one was rushing to the rescue. And when the person in the room moaned again, Mina decided it was up to her to see if they needed help.

As she stepped into the room, a baby blue privacy curtain blocked her view. Mina reached up, started to pull it back, then paused.

"Hello?" She waited. Another moan. "I don't work here. I was here with—" She stopped herself. What did it matter to the person behind the curtain why she was here and why volunteer unnecessary information? Instead, she went with, "Do you need help?"

What a stupid question, she thought even before the words stopped spilling from her mouth. The machine doesn't make that sound if things are okay. And people don't moan like that unless they're in trouble.

Mina pulled back the curtain, and the first thing she saw was the nurse who'd instructed her to wait with her dead father. The beautiful woman was sprawled on the floor beside the empty hospital bed.

Her once pristine pink scrubs were now shredded and stained with blood. Most of her flesh was missing. Even the bones showed through in places. To Mina, the nurse looked like she'd taken a dip in a pool filled with piranhas.

A wet, gasping noise from the bathroom at the other end of the room drew Mina's attention away from the dead nurse. Mina approached the half-closed door.

What are you doing, you ding dong? It was her father's voice she heard echoing through her head. *You ain't got many brains, but it's time you used 'em. Get your ass out of here before it's too late.*

"Shut up!" she hissed and didn't realize she'd said it aloud until a gagging gurgle answered from the bathroom.

"Hey," she said to the half-closed door. "Do you want me to get someone?"

When she didn't get an answer, Mina gritted her teeth and pushed the door open. What she saw was even more of a shock than her dead father attacking her.

The small, Indian doctor who had pronounced her father dead sat upright, his back against the blue tiled bathroom wall. His head hung limp and his chin rested on his chest. At the doctor's midsection, Mina saw an old woman in a hospital gown on her hands and knees. The gown had ridden up, and the split flapped open to reveal her saggy, wrinkled ass. The old woman's face was buried in the doctor's stomach, her head twisting back and forth as she burrowed into his bowels.

The sour aroma of shit hit Mina as violently as her father's fist, and she couldn't hold back a dry retch. That drew the attention of the old woman, who pulled back and her face came free of the doctor's innards with a sloppy sucking sound. *Schwock!*

Blood and bits of intestines covered the woman, and when she saw Mina, the woman scrambled to her feet and loped toward her.

Mina slammed the door into the woman. It bounced off her, and the old zombie stumbled backward and tripped over the doctor's body. Mina dashed away from the bathroom, but footsteps resumed behind her, and they were coming faster than Mina could run.

She spotted an aluminum cane propped against the nightstand by the bed and grabbed it. She spun around. The old woman was just a step away, blood and feces seeping from her open jaws as she growled.

Mina's instincts took over, and when the old woman got within arm's reach, she slammed the butt end of the cane into the zombie's face. She felt teeth break as the shaft smashed through them, and, for a brief moment, the zombie stood there with the gray metal jutting from her mouth like the world's biggest straw.

Then, she snapped her head back and gave no indication that the shattered remains of her front teeth affected her in the slightest. She yanked the cane free of her mouth, tossed it aside, and dove toward Mina. The two collapsed in a heap, and the thing that had once been human was on top.

It growled and bared what remained of its teeth and red saliva hung in thick ropes, which dripped onto Mina's face. Mina turned her head just in time to prevent them from landing in her mouth.

She's like a rabid dog, Mina thought. Then, as if to prove the point, the old woman snapped at her and came within half an inch of biting her face. So close that Mina could smell the fetid aroma of intestines on the zombie's breath.

Mina pushed against the old woman's throat, held her at bay, and reached for the fallen cane with her free hand. The zombie kept biting and clawing at her until a shriek pierced the air and stole the monster's attention.

Mina wanted to look away, to look for the source of the scream, but the thing atop her was distracted, and she knew this was her best chance. Maybe her only chance.

Mina grabbed the cane. Pinned against the floor, she knew she wouldn't be able to build enough momentum to get any force behind a swing, but she had another idea. As soon as the old woman looked back down at her, Mina rammed the bottom of the cane up and into the woman's left eye. It gave a muffled pop, and then the shaft sunk deeper into the zombie's skull. There was a small crunch as the eye socket broke, and soon after, the old woman went limp.

Mina squirmed out from underneath the dead weight, trying to avoid the muck and carnage but only half succeeding. Once she worked herself free, she fled the room.

The hallway, which had been empty just a few minutes earlier—minutes that felt like hours—now contained a dozen zombies, all fighting to get a bite out of a chubby janitor. He tried to fight them off with his mop, but they overwhelmed him. His wash bucket fell over in the struggle and his spilled blood mixed with the soapy water and pink foam ebbed out in shallow waves.

Mina raced in the opposite direction, toward the elevator doors. As she ran, she passed the nurse's station where two zombie RNs were fighting a young male orderly. One of the women pulled the man's face toward her own, and their mouths met. The nurse bit down on his lips and, in one hard bite, tore them clean off. Mina kept running, and the nurse who wasn't eating the man's face gave chase.

Mina couldn't stop fast enough to avoid hitting the closed elevator doors and knocked the wind out of herself. The number 4 glowed above the elevator. Just one floor away. She smashed the down arrow, which flickered yellow. She pressed it again and again, as if that would make any difference.

Footsteps, several sets of footsteps, closed in on her. Mina refused to look back, even when they were so near that she could feel the floor vibrating under her feet. They growled and snarled and gasped, and still, she wouldn't look.

Then, with a cheerful ding, the elevator doors opened. Mina dove through as soon as the gap was wide enough to accept her slender frame. Her foot caught in the space between the hallway and the elevator floor, and she tumbled to her knees.

She turned around, fumbling to hit the "Door close" button. She missed on the first try but connected with the second, and again, she waited. Only this time, she looked at what was coming. More than twenty zombies now dashed down the hallway. Amongst them was the little Indian doctor who she'd seen being eaten a short time ago. His open gut spilled intestines, which trailed behind him like streamers on a "Just married" limo.

The zombies were fifteen feet away. Eight. Five.

The doors groaned and started to close but slowly.

Three feet.

The zombies were almost within arm's reach. She could hear their wet, hungry vocalizations. The horrible sounds drowned out everything else. They strained for the gap between the elevator doors.

And the doors closed.

Muzak played over the elevator speakers. Mina collapsed into the corner and tried to keep her composure. She recognized the tune as an off-key version of *Blue Bayou*.

CHAPTER THIRTY-THREE

AFTER A DAY OF KILLING, almost being killed, and a restless night's sleep during which he suffered through nightmares of both, Wim woke up lacking any motivation. He considered abandoning his plan to exterminate the zombies which had replaced his onetime neighbors.

Truth be told, he didn't know any of them all that well when he was alive, and he wondered why it was now his duty to clean up the mess.

That internal debate lasted the better part of an hour before he accepted the fact that destroying the monsters wasn't simply the moral thing to do but the humane thing. Letting them go on would be no different than allowing a lame animal to suffer. And as hard as he liked to believe he could be when the situation necessitated it, one thing he was not was cruel.

In the kitchen, he grabbed a loaf of bread he'd been working on since before the zombies and found it covered with a light dusting of mold. He scraped off as much as he could, then slathered it in strawberry jam. He only got down two mouthfuls before he realized he had no appetite. After reloading all of his firearms, he was on the road.

When he reached town, another two dozen or so zombies had made it into the streets. He killed them all, then dragged their bodies into the empty corner lot where the funeral home used to stand before a tornado knocked it down in the 90s.

Once the streets were again clear, Wim moved from house to house. Like in many small towns, most people left their doors unlocked, and he was free to enter without much fuss. Each time, he prayed he'd find someone alive, but those prayers went unanswered. A few homes were empty, but most housed zombies.

The worst was the Lohr residence. It was a pretty yellow Victorian with a white picket fence in front, and Wim always thought it looked like it belonged on a postcard.

When he entered, he found Cathy and Stu Lohr roaming the downstairs. Stu looked normal enough for a zombie, but Cathy had several small chunks of flesh taken out of her arms and face, which looked a little like oversized chicken pox.

When they saw him, they lurched in his direction, grumbling or growling or whatever the heck sounds these things made. Wim put them both down, and when his ears stopped ringing after the gunshots, he heard more movement upstairs. He climbed the carpeted stairs and what he found when he got to the landing horrified him.

The Lohr's were a fertile family, and they had five children, four girls and one boy, all under the age of ten. The youngest was under a year old and wasn't walking yet. He was the first one Wim saw.

The baby was at the top of the steps, crawling on his hands and knees. He wore nothing but a saggy, stained cloth diaper. Blood was smeared all over his little face and mouth.

He saw Wim and tried to maneuver down the stairs, but when his torso dropped over the top step, he somersaulted forward, and momentum carried him down to the landing. The baby landed on its back and it looked up and backward at Wim and clawed at the air with its tiny hands. Wim couldn't look as he raised his heavy, steel-toed boot, the kind his Mama always called 'shit stompers' and brought it down on the tot's skull. It crumpled like an empty soda can.

He continued up the stairs and reached the second floor. There were four rooms. The first he checked was the parents' bedroom and found it empty. The second was the nursery. It, too, was empty, but something had upended the crib.

Wim was halfway down the hall and there was a doorway on each side of him. He checked the room to his right first, and inside he discovered two of the girls sitting on the floor. It looked like there was a doll in front of them, but as Wim moved closer, he saw it was one of their sisters, or rather, what remained of her.

They had eaten the little girl's arms and legs down to the bone. A cavernous hole where the organs had once been marred her torso. All the skin on her face was gone, revealing a jigsaw of muscle and tendon underneath. Her lidless eyes held nothing but empty black sockets. It reminded Wim of a video cover he'd seen in the rental store once for *The Incredible Melting Man*.

Wim shot the first girl in the back of the head. As she tumbled forward like a rag doll, her sister lunged at Wim and caught hold of his right arm. He tried to shake her off, but the girl had a firm grip on his shirtsleeve.

When he grabbed a fistful of her blonde hair with his left hand, she glared at him and snarled. He could see bits of flesh stuck between her baby teeth and she bit at him like a snapping turtle.

Wim whipped her head back and forth until she let loose of his shirt, then threw her down on the floor. She tried to get up, but he held her down with his foot. She looked up at him as the bullet blew through her forehead.

He didn't have time to turn around before the last of the Lohr children was on him. The little monster jumped onto his back and scratched at his head and neck.

Wim threw himself backwards into the wall and the girl lost her grip and fell off. As he turned to her, she ran at him and he saw small bites on her face and neck. He had no time to aim the pistol as she dashed toward him, so much quicker and more agile than the others, and his first shot caught her in the throat. Blood beaded up in the hollow between her collarbones. She stumbled backward a step then rushed toward him again.

He fired again, and this time, the bullet collided with the space between her nose and her left eye and blood exploded out the back of her skull and splattered against the wall behind her. She dropped in a heap. It was done.

Wim took their bodies to the empty lot. The little ones were so small he could carry three on one trip and two on the other.

He continued on until he'd checked every house in town. He found no one alive, but plenty of the undead, and by the time he'd dragged all the bodies to the pile it was nearly three feet high and forty feet from end to end. He hadn't kept an accurate count, but knew he'd killed over two hundred zombies.

At the only gas station in town, the pumps were useless due to the electricity being out, so Wim took a big fifty-five gallon drum of used motor oil and rolled it up the street. Once he got it to the edge of the pile, he stood the barrel upright, then rocked it until it fell onto the bodies.

He pushed it as close to the center as he could, crawling over the men and women he'd killed, then popped the top. Thick, black muck seeped out and Wim grabbed some old rags he'd taken from the garage and plugged the opening before too much could escape.

He then lit the clothing of some of the bodies nearest the drum on fire and scrambled off the pile as the flames caught hold. Wim trudged back to his truck, which he'd parked a hundred yards away, and grabbed his Marlin. He waited until the flames had spread out, their yellow tips licking the air, then aimed the rifle at the barrel.

The first shot sent a wave of fire to the right. The second splashed burning oil into the air and rained down over the zombies like hail in a spring storm. Wim figured that was enough to do the job, and by the time he'd finished loading the guns back into his truck, the entire mound was aflame.

Black smoke billowed into the air as the pyre burned higher and hotter. Wim sat in his truck and stared at the flames through the windshield. It occurred to him that he'd killed just about everyone he'd ever known. He still had to check the homes and farms outside of town, but there, he'd most likely have to kill the rest.

It was all too much. He couldn't do any more killing today. He leaned against the steering wheel, the orange light of the fire turning his face into a Jack-o'-lantern, and sobbed.

CHAPTER THIRTY-FOUR

BUNDY HAD DITCHED the car half an hour earlier. He needed something with more room, both for his body and for what he hoped to find. He wanted an SUV, the bigger the better, but when he came across a bright blue Caravan, he figured it would do.

The driver's side door hung ajar and the engine idled smoothly. An arc of red blood decorated the interior of the windshield, and it was easy to infer that nothing good had happened here. When he climbed inside, he spotted a rear-facing child's car seat in the back. He checked and was relieved it was empty and undisturbed.

Bundy tossed the car seat into the grassy median. The highway was all but abandoned. The few vehicles that traveled the road were forced to go slow to avoid the abandoned cars and the zombies which roamed about, seeking a fresh meal.

There weren't many. In the hour Bundy had been driving, he'd only seen fifteen or twenty, but the general emptiness of the interstate made it clear enough that things had gone sour, and it had happened fast.

Bundy left the keys in the VW but shut off the engine so that there'd be gas for whoever might come along next. He considered writing a note to tell them where he was heading but decided against it. Bundy possessed a trusting disposition, one which landed him in prison, and he figured it might be time to be more cautious.

He drove almost ninety miles toward his pre-prison hometown. He had no interest in going home. His parents were dead, and there was no sentimentality when it came to his four-room apartment. But there was one important stop to make.

Uneeda Storage Unit stood a few miles outside of town. The squat white garages filled an otherwise vacant industrial desert, their metal roofs were blinding in the sunlight. Bundy steered the van into the lot, which, as expected, was unlocked (Open 24/7/365!) and didn't stop until he was in front of unit 317.

When he confirmed the padlock he'd used to protect his storage unit was undisturbed, Bundy gave a low whistle. He'd rented the unit under the name "Colt Springfield," which he had found amusing at the time, but after his arrest, he thought it might have been a little too clever for his own good. But with the lock still in place, it seemed his subterfuge had been a success.

The facility was empty of people, which was a relief because Bundy had no key to his locker. He used a four-way lug wrench from the van's trunk to beat the padlock into submission. The lock itself held, but the surrounding metal of the door gave way, and it clattered to the ground with a satisfying *clack*.

Bundy took a moment to catch his breath. He never minded being fat, but it made any kind of physical exertion much more tiring than necessary. After a brief period of recuperation, he bent at the waist, grabbed the handle, and raised the garage door. Daylight spilled inside and revealed a cube of neatly stacked cardboard boxes, each labeled with things like "Kitchen," "Clothes," and "Misc." in Bundy's simple printing.

Fortunately, some of the boxes marked as clothes actually did contain clothing because Bundy was eager to shed his fluorescent orange jumpsuit. His days of being Inmate 2089349 were over, and, besides, that jumpsuit was too damned hot.

He stripped off everything but his socks, then opened a box. He took out a pair of boxer shorts, a plain black tank top, and a pair of jeans so large he could only order them online. Before he could redress, he heard the scraping of feet against the macadam outside.

"Son of a bitch," Bundy said as he let the clothing fall to the cement floor of the storage unit.

He pulled open a cardboard box upon which "Photo albums" was written. Inside, buried amongst a sea of white Styrofoam peanuts, was an admirable cache of handguns. He grabbed a pearl-handled Colt pistol, then moved to a box labeled "knick knacks." Ammunition packed that box. As he searched for .380 ammo, the scraping sound outside the unit grew louder and nearer.

Bundy found box after box of bullets for .44s, .357s, and 9mm, but .380s eluded him.

"Screw it," he said as he traded the pistol for a box of .44s. As he returned to the box of guns, he realized the footsteps had stopped. Bundy stood there, naked as a newborn baby but about sixty times larger, and listened.

Maybe it's a person, he thought, although he doubted that. A person would have said something. Bundy could feel a presence behind him. He didn't hear breathing or feel any body heat, but something was there. Something was close.

He felt like his balls had been sucked up into his gut, and it took every bit of mental fortitude he possessed to turn around.

The zombie that stood before him appeared to have been an old woman. Her face had been eaten away, but wild clumps of bloodied gray hair jutted from her head. She stood no more than five feet tall, well under a foot and a half shorter than Bundy. When she lunged at him, she bounced off his amply padded chest.

Before he could react, he felt her biting him, the slimy wetness of her mouth against his flesh. He grabbed on to her hair and jerked her head back. He held her at arm's length as he looked down at his skin, where he saw blood smeared against his nipple, but he couldn't see a wound.

He examined the zombie, then gazed at her mouth and saw that its withered old gums held no teeth.

A relieved, almost giddy smile broke out on his broad face. An eternity wandering around as a fat, naked zombie would have been a horrible, final joke in a life where he'd all too frequently been the punch line.

"Guess you picked the wrong time to run out of Polident, you old hag."

She hissed and clawed at him, but her frail dead body was easy to hold back. Bundy shoved her away from him, and the zombie tumbled over a few of the boxes. While she climbed back to her feet, Bundy moved to the edge of the storage unit and grabbed the lug wrench. No use wasting a bullet. He had a feeling he'd need every last one.

The old woman was up again and coming at him when Bundy swung the lug wrench and connected with her forehead. The metal broke an almost perfect hole in her skull, and when she fell to the floor, bits of black blood and gray brain matter trickled from the wound.

Bundy looked outside again, scanning the area for zombies. Once convinced he was alone, he dressed. Then he loaded all the handguns to capacity and placed them in the van. He added two large and heavy boxes labeled "4th of July decorations." He didn't know if he'd need the contents, but it couldn't hurt. Well, it could hurt. Quite a bit if he wasn't careful.

He longed for the rest of his collection, which he had kept locked away in heavy-duty gun safes at his apartment, but the feds confiscated all of them after his conviction. No guns for felons, after all. They were dangerous. He found himself longing for the Hellpup that got him sent away. Whoever said the average American had no need for automatic weapons never had to deal with zombies.

CHAPTER THIRTY-FIVE

AFTER HER MOTHER'S police blotter fame had turned them both into local pariahs, Ramey grew to hate the town in which she'd grown up. The town in which she'd elected to stay rather than run away to greener pastures with her father. Still, as she drove the pickup down the streets and saw the destruction taking place, she couldn't help but feel nostalgic.

The Glow n Bowl bowling alley where she'd had her thirteenth birthday party was on fire and was sending dirty gray clouds into the sky, like smoke signals calling for help that wouldn't come. Several figures, which Ramey judged to be preteens from their size, stumbled about the parking lot. Despite their charred black skin, they seemed beyond pain.

When a woman in a housecoat with cartoon kitten prints came running down the sidewalk, the burned zombies caught on to her presence and moved in her direction. Ramey drove toward her, and, as she got closer, she saw the woman was Mrs. Kraft, her third-grade teacher.

"Get in!" Ramey yelled.

The teacher glanced at Ramey with feverish, bloodshot eyes and showed no sign of recognizing her former student.

"Mrs. Kraft, get in the truck!"

The woman looked away from Ramey and toward the burned child zombies.

"Zeke?" she called out. "Zeke? It's Mommy."

Shit, her son must be one of those charbroiled ghouls, Ramey thought. The zombies were now only a few yards away. She shouted again at her teacher. "They're dead! Can't you see that? Come with me!"

Mrs. Kraft didn't move to the truck or flee from the zombies. Instead, she ran toward them. How she could tell which of the crispy critters was her Zeke was a mystery to Ramey, but the woman picked out one in red Pumas and embraced it.

The boy took a heaping mouthful of tit, like a baby well past its feeding time, and bit right through the kitten housecoat. He pulled away a bloody chunk of flesh as Mrs. Kraft screamed and cried. Then the other deep-fried zombies joined the party. Ramey didn't wait—she'd seen enough—and the tires squealed as she sped away.

She tried to focus only on the road as she drove off, but her peripheral vision revealed the descent into chaos. When the "Thanks for visiting. Come back real soon!" sign appeared at the border, she felt a mixture of relief and regret, and she knew without a doubt she'd never see her hometown again. No great loss.

The dilapidated storefronts and warehouses disappeared from her rear-view mirror, and the landscape switched to fields and forests. After a few miles of seeing no zombies (no humans either), she began to relax.

For the past year, a part of Ramey thought her dreams of running away were only that, dreams. And the voice inside her head said she would end up pregnant to some dimwit like Bobby Mack, waiting tables at the truck stop and spending her tips on scratch off tickets because they'd be her only chance of escape.

Even worse, the voice told her she would end up like her mother. Just another former pretty face wasting her life and a sore back away from a pill addiction. But now, she was out, even if the circumstances were unexpected and undesirable.

Ramey did know where to go, and her mind flitted between thoughts of the past and thoughts of the future. If there would even be a future. The #zombiepresident trending topic she had seen just before the internet evaporated kept coming to mind. If that was true, the entire country was in trouble. The whole world. And if the world was screwed, where did that leave that was safe?

Safe… The word made her think of her father's letter.

It's safe here.

Was it? She had her doubts. She loved her father, but he was a hopeless dreamer, always prattling about what a great world was out there if people could stop chasing money and focus on each other. Peace and love and all that hippy dippy bullshit. The kind of things that sounded great but ignored the fact that, deep down, most people suck. But still, she wondered, could he be somewhere safe?

Her hand went to her pocket, and she felt the folds of the letter through the denim of her jeans. She reached to grab the paper and looked away from the road. In doing so, she didn't see the jack-knifed big rig ahead of her. And she didn't see the three zombies milling around the cab.

Ramey extracted the letter and map from her too-skinny skinny jeans, then looked up and saw the tractor trailer blocking both lanes of the country road. She was only yards away, and it took a few seconds for the shock to pass before she hit her brakes.

That wasn't enough time to stop. In the blurry confusion of surprise, Ramey couldn't even tell that the two men and one woman in the roadway were already quite dead, so she jerked the wheel hard to the left.

The lifted pickup swayed and felt almost like it was floating. The feeling you have on a roller coaster when you crest the peak and plunge down the opposite side.

She realized the truck was on the verge of flipping over, so she eased the wheel out of the too-sharp turn. The pickup stabilized, but in the process, she slammed into one of the men standing in the road, hitting him in the back. He flipped in mid-air before flopping onto the pavement.

The woman closest to him was next in Ramey's path. That one turned toward the truck at the last second, and Ramey saw the zombie was missing an eye and half its cheek, so she didn't feel bad when she hit it straight on. That creature performed no gymnastics. It fell straight back, and Ramey heard it crunch under the passenger side tires.

The resistance, coupled with Ramey braking, brought the truck to a halt a few feet before it could smash into the eighteen-wheeler.

"Jesus Christ!" Ramey said to herself.

She backed up and felt more bones snap under the weight of the beefy mud tires, then surveyed the scene. One zombie remained standing. It had been an elderly, balding man with shocks of white hair popping out from the sides of its head like a geriatric circus clown.

Ramey considered running it over, but she didn't know how much more the old pickup could take. As she prepared to drive off and let it be, a noise caught her attention. Was that a voice?

She rolled down her window, leaned out, and listened.

"I'm stuck in here!"

Yep, it was a voice, and Ramey wasn't the only one who heard it. Zombie Bozo had too, and the monster staggered toward the cab of the trailer, which laid toppled on its side.

"Damn it." Ramey exited the safety of her own ride but not before grabbing the lug wrench which laid on the seat.

The old zombie focused only on the voice in the big rig and missed Ramey coming up from behind. She swung the metal rod, and the fat end connected with the creature's skull. There was a light cracking sound like Ramey had stepped on a potato chip. The zombie stopped walking and did a slow-motion fall to the roadway. It stayed down.

"You're a pistol!" the voice inside the big rig called out.

Ramey stepped to the truck and looked through the windshield. Daylight reflected off the glass and made it hard to see inside, but when she leaned in close, she could make out the silhouette of a man behind the wheel.

"How are you stuck?" Ramey asked.

"Damn seatbelt's all twisted around me and jammed. Been in here for over four hours!"

Ramey returned to the pickup and grabbed a pocket knife that had been laying in a cubby on the dash. She went back to the tractor trailer.

The cab was driver's side down and stood a few feet taller than Ramey. She didn't relish the thought of trying to climb on top to reach the passenger side door.

"I've got a knife. Now, how do I get it to you?"

"Bust out the windshield," the man said.

Ramey paused. "Are you sure?"

"Hell yes, I'm sure. This big ol' bitch ain't going anywhere anytime soon, anyway."

Ramey got close to the front windshield. She raised the lug wrench, reared back, then hesitated.

"Cover your eyes." She watched the driver hold his hands over his face. Satisfied, she swung. A small divot appeared in the bug-splattered glass, but that was all.

"Again!" he said.

She swung again, this time using even more force than she'd used on the zombie. She connected at about the same spot, and a dozen thin lines spider-webbed out from the point of impact.

"One more oughta do it!" he said.

Ramey sighed. Each blow sent painful shocks up her arms, and her hands felt numb and shaky. She swung again, and the spider-webs turned into a mosaic with a fat hole in the middle. It was big enough to fit her arm through, and the safety glass posed little harm as she passed the knife through to the driver.

He cut the seatbelt, and Ramey heard a thud as he fell a few inches into the door below him. He grunted and swore, then asked for the lug wrench, which she was glad to hand over. From the inside, he broke apart the windshield until there was a man-sized opening. He slithered through it head first, and Ramey had to fight away a smile when she thought it looked like the cab was giving birth to him.

The man was around forty-five or fifty, Ramey guessed, and skinny. He wasn't much taller than she was, and she didn't break five feet three inches unless she wore boots. He had a Patriots cap parked atop his head and a tag on his shirt declaring his name to be Stan.

"I'm Stan," he confirmed.

"I gathered as much," Ramey said, pointing to his shirt.

"Oh. Yeah." He handed her the knife and the lug wrench. "Thanks for the help, Miss. I was up shit creek, that's for sure."

"I think we all are."

He thought about that for a moment, then nodded. "Yeah. Before the C.B. went off, it sure sounded that way." Stan looked at the dead things on the ground. "They're zombies, aren't they?"

Ramey shrugged her shoulders. "I don't know what else you'd call them."

Stan looked up the road toward town, then down the road in the direction Ramey had been going before they met.

"Where are you headed?"

She thought about that, about her father and his letter and map. She knew the odds were slim, but what else was out there?

"I was thinking about here." She handed Stan the map.

He examined it for a moment, then nodded. "What's there?"

"My dad. Maybe."

"I've been in that general vicinity a few times. It's a few hundred miles from here. Not the best roads, though. Want me to come along with?"

Ramey looked at the wiry little man with his craggy face and wide eyes. He looked harmless, but then again, most people do during the day when the light casts shadows that hide all of their secrets.

"Don't you have anyone you want to check on?" she asked.

Stan shook his head. "Been divorced going on ten years. No kiddos. My parents are long gone." He gave a bashful grin. "There's a girl I see when I'm in Memphis, but that's only a couple times a year. Besides, I suspect she's got some other fella friends, if you catch my drift."

His cheeks turned bright pink and his eyes darted to the ground, and she knew then that she could trust him. Besides, Stan traveled for a living, and she'd never been more than fifty miles away from home, and it seemed they'd make a good team.

"Well then, let's do it."

He looked up, and his grin turned into a full smile, which, although it revealed a few holes where teeth should have been, was downright charming.

"Great! Let me just get something from my rig."

He climbed back into the cab and emerged a few moments later with the prize. A silver Ruger revolver, which possessed what looked to Ramey an obnoxiously long barrel.

"Figure this might come in handy," he said as he looked down at the zombies.

"Good call, Stan."

She started for her truck. Even if she had stolen it, it was hers now.

"What's your name?" Stan asked as he jogged to catch up.

"Ramey," she said as she climbed into the driver's seat. "Now, I'll drive, and you navigate."

"Sounds like a plan."

She drove into the grass, which licked at the tires as she steered around Stan's wrecked rig, then pulled back onto the rural road. Ahead, the coast was clear.

CHAPTER THIRTY-SIX

A HIGH-PITCHED WHISTLING sound woke Grady from a deep sleep. The shrill noise filled his bedroom. Is that a fire whistle? It sounds so close.

He fumbled for the lamp on the nightstand and, after a few moments of searching, found the switch. The 40-watt bulb cast dim light into the dreary room, and Grady looked toward the window, expecting to see the flashing signs of fire trucks. He saw nothing, but the whistle continued. What is that?

He sat up, and the worn-out quilt he'd received from his grandmother as a wedding present slid down his torso. He swung his legs off the bed and wiped the last vestiges of sleep from his eyes as he approached the window.

Before he reached it, he realized the sound was not coming from outside. It was coming from his living room/kitchen. That's when he realized Josiah wasn't in the single bed that sat tight against his own double.

Grady rushed out of the bedroom and found his son sprawled on his back on the living room floor. He dropped to his knees, skinning them on the carpet and ignoring the burning pain from the exposed nerves. Josiah's hands were at his throat, and his tiny fingers had scratched long gashes down his neck. Air struggled its way in and out of his mouth.

Oh, God, no. Please, God, I can't lose him. Anything but that.

Grady tilted the boy's head back, then pulled open his mouth and tried to look inside for something blocking his airway. He saw nothing. Josiah's eyes had rolled so far back that almost nothing but white showed.

"Josiah? Can you hear me? Can you hear Daddy?"

The boy had never spoken a word in his short life. Grady knew that, but it was all he could think to say. Josiah only kept wheezing.

Grady grabbed the telephone off the wall and punched nine and one before he realized there was no dial tone. He hung it up, then took it again. The line was dead. He tapped the switch hook, not knowing why, but people always did it in the movies, so there must be a reason. It made no difference.

Please, Jesus Christ in Heaven, protect my boy. Embrace him in your healing arms.

Grady dropped the phone and rushed back to his son. He scooped the boy up in his arms and ran to the apartment door. After unlocking it, he raced out of the apartment and into the black, night air. He didn't even realize he'd forgotten to put on shoes until he felt the wet grass under his feet, but that was okay; he didn't need shoes. He needed to save his son.

Grady sprinted down the sidewalk. The streets were empty of everything except litter. He had no idea what time it was. It could be 11 p.m. or 5 a.m., and, as he headed for the bus stop, he realized the next bus could be hours away.

Three blocks later, he discovered the bus stop vacant. The glass cubicle that had once provided shelter from bad weather was shattered. That wasn't too unusual, but Grady could also see dark, wet blood smeared against the green bench that sat amongst the destruction. He couldn't allow himself to think about what might have happened there. He needed help. His son needed help.

Please, Jesus, protect him.

Josiah's whistling wheezes had decreased in frequency as Grady ran. They now came only once every five or six seconds. Sometimes, half a minute passed in between them. And as they waited for a bus that might never come, his breathing stopped altogether.

It took Grady a moment to realize Josiah wasn't going to breathe again on his own, so when he did, his mind exploded in confused, distraught thoughts. Why is this happening? What's wrong with him? How can I get him help? What should I do? Why is this happening to us, God?

That last thought snapped him out of his panic. God helps those who help themselves.

He released Josiah from his tight embrace and laid the boy out on the safety glass-covered sidewalk. He used his fingers to open Josiah's mouth again, but this time he didn't look inside. Instead, he pressed his own mouth over his son's and breathed. He sent five big breaths into the boy's lungs, then waited.

Nothing.

He gave five more breaths. Then ten. Still, the boy refused to breathe on his own.

"You can't take my boy!" Grady screamed, and the sound of his own voice startled him. He hadn't spoken above a whisper in years, and he couldn't remember shouting since he was a boy, and that was playing games and in fun. This was pain and anger, and it felt like something had burst open inside him.

"God, don't do this! Don't take him from me!"

Tears streamed from Grady's eyes and rained down onto Josiah's small, vacant face.

"What you going on about?" a man's voice said.

Grady spun around and saw a black man in a Ravens skullcap. He seemed vaguely familiar, and Grady remembered seeing him in the shadows of the street and under stoops trading baggies for cash.

Before, Grady had tried not to notice him, to ignore the gangster dealing drugs, but in the ghastly glow of the arc sodium streetlight, he could see the man was younger than he'd earlier thought. He might not even be twenty. Heavy gold chains sagged down from his neck and more gold adorned his ears and lip. The grip of a pistol jutted out above the crotch of his jeans.

"You speak English or what?" the man asked Grady.

"It's my son." Grady looked down to Josiah, then back to the gangster. "He's sick. He's having trouble breathing."

"So, call an ambulance, man."

"My phone was out. And I don't have a car."

The man grabbed a cell phone from his pocket, dialed, listened, and frowned, staring at the phone.

"All circuits are busy. What the fuck that mean?"

Grady reached out and grabbed hold of the man's baggy jeans. "Please. Please, help us. My son's going to die without help."

The man looked down at Josiah as he pocketed his phone. He then stared up and down the empty street. "All right, man. All right. You wait here."

He jogged away. Grady watched him disappear behind a row house, then resumed breathing into his son's mouth. Less than two minutes later, a black seventies Lincoln Continental with obnoxiously large chrome rims roared to a stop in front of them.

The passenger side window rolled down, and the gangster banged his hand against the door. "Yo, man! What you waitin' for?"

Grady grabbed Josiah under his knees and shoulders and lifted him into the backseat of the Lincoln, then climbed in beside his son.

A different man was driving. He, too, was black and about the same age but much larger. Long coarse dreadlocks tumbled down his plus-sized head. He didn't say a word as Grady sat down. He only stared.

"That's O'Dell. He don't say much. But this is his ride."

"Thank you so much. You're a Godsend."

O'Dell only nodded. As soon as Grady pulled the door shut, Odell hit the gas, and the Lincoln sped away.

———

A WRECK ON 40 BLOCKED THE ENTIRE STREET. GRADY COULD SEE A Cadillac Escalade flipped on its roof and a smoking Dodge pickup with a crushed hood only a few feet away. Despite the crashed vehicles, he saw no one.

He gave it little thought as he clutched Josiah tight. He felt the coldness taking over the boy's body but refused to admit it to himself. He continued giving breath after breath. Soon, he'll breathe again. I believe it. I have faith. God won't take my boy.

O'Dell made a hard left onto a side street, almost throwing Grady and his son off the seat. The original gangster, who had identified himself as LaRon, glanced into the backseat.

"Hold tight back there. How's he doing?"

Grady didn't meet his eyes. "He'll be okay. Just please get us to the hospital."

LaRon looked down at Josiah. "We're getting there, little man. You hang on."

After a few more turns, LaRon called out, "Almost there," and just as he did, Josiah opened his eyes.

Grady gasped. He put his hands on Josiah's chest—so cold—and tried to feel it rise and fall. He couldn't feel anything, but the boy's eyes were open, and they looked at him. Grady raised his son up and embraced him so hard he worried he'd injure the boy, but he couldn't stop himself.

Thank, God. Thank you, God!

Josiah squirmed and struggled against Grady's grasp, and now afraid that he had hurt his son, Grady let him loose. The boy looked around the car, then caught sight of the driver.

Before Grady knew what was happening, Josiah lunged forward, tumbling off Grady's lap. He caught hold of one of O'Dell's dreads on the way down and yanked the man's head sideways.

The car swerved to the right, then O'Dell pulled the wheel to the left to regain control. Grady tried to pull Josiah's hand free of the gangster's hair but couldn't break his grip. The boy used his other hand to claw at O'Dell's face. He pulled himself toward the driver, their faces just inches apart, then bit the side of the man's ear off.

"Motherfuck!" O'Dell yelled.

Grady didn't have time to process what had just happened before the front wheels bounced over a curb. There was a loud crash as the grill of the Lincoln slammed into a row of steel newspaper machines on the sidewalk. The sudden halt threw them all forward. At last, Josiah let go of the dreadlock.

O'Dell threw open his door and jumped out of the car. He then threw open the back door, grabbed Grady, and dragged him out of the Continental. Grady slammed into the sidewalk and felt a rib break.

LaRon exited the car from the passenger seat. He was so worked up that he bounced on his feet like a jumping bean.

"Your fucking kid bit him!" LaRon said.

O'Dell held his hand against his bleeding ear.

"He's sick," Grady said.

"No shit he's sick! What the fuck he got? Rabies?" LaRon said.

O'Dell dove into the car after the boy. Grady tried to jump up, but a jolt in his ribcage dropped him back to his knees. He watched the gangster grab his son by his frog pajamas and pull him from the car. He tossed Josiah like a rag doll, and the child slammed into the ground in front of his father.

Grady tried to grab Josiah, to hold him close and protect him, but the second the boy hit the ground, he was back on his feet and moving toward O'Dell.

"You best control that bitch!" O'Dell yelled. It was only the second time he'd spoken since Grady and Josiah had climbed into the car and rage filled his voice.

Grady reached for Josiah again, but he was just out of reach. Grady struggled to his feet and stumbled toward Josiah, who was still heading for the big gangster.

O'Dell held out his arm to block the boy, but Josiah dove for his hand and caught the fatty hunk of flesh between his thumb and forefinger in his teeth. The gangster's eyes grew wide, and Grady saw blood.

The gangster screamed and jerked his hand free. He ignored the blood and pulled the pistol from his jeans and aimed it at Josiah's head.

"No!" Grady screamed. "Don't. Don't shoot him!" He grabbed his son and tried to shield him. Why is this happening? God had just given him back his son, he couldn't take him away again. It wasn't fair.

O'Dell pulled back the slide to chamber a round, and Grady sobbed. The boy struggled against him, but this time Grady held on.

LaRon grabbed onto O'Dell's meaty, tattooed arm, the one holding the gun, and pulled it down. "It's just a kid, man."

O'Dell glared at him, then returned the pistol to his jeans. He jumped back into his wrecked Lincoln and threw it in reverse. The tires squealed as it pulled loose from the newspaper boxes and bounced back onto the street. Then he drove away.

LaRon watched him go, then turned back to the crying father and his biting son.

Grady loosened his grip on Josiah. He saw the boy was eating the flesh he'd bitten off O'Dell. Grady's stomach did a cartwheel, and, a second later, the remains of his hamburger helper dinner landed on the sidewalk.

Josiah swallowed the skin, then tried to pull free of Grady, who held on.

"No!" Grady ordered.

Before that moment, Josiah never seemed to hear a word he said, but now he looked up at his father and stopped squirming. The boy held out his hand, and Grady took it in his own.

"Crazy fuckin' white people," LaRon said, then turned away from them and jogged up the street.

Grady ignored his exit. He was entranced by the way his son looked at him. Josiah was seeing him for the first time ever.

"Josiah? Are you okay?"

The boy gave a wet gasp that came out like "Ah-bah," but Grady heard, "Da da." He embraced his son, and the boy didn't pull away. Grady kissed his cold cheek and tears streamed from his eyes. He couldn't remember being that happy in years. God hadn't just answered his prayers; he'd performed a miracle.

They walked down the sidewalk, hand in hand, both still in their nightclothes and shoeless. Grady thought gripping Josiah's hand was like holding a piece of raw chicken that had been recently removed from the refrigerator. Somewhere inside, he knew the boy was dead. But that didn't matter.

This was the miracle he'd been praying for. God had saved Josiah, and now Grady was prepared to do whatever God asked of him.

CHAPTER THIRTY-SEVEN

MITCH DARTED his tongue in and out of Rochelle's beautiful pussy, which, as far as he believed, was more perfect than anything Michelangelo himself could have sculpted. It tasted like strawberries, and he could have stayed between her toned legs forever. Then she coughed. Her body convulsed and her thighs bucked, pushing his mouth away from her groin. When he looked up, he saw her face had gone blue, starved of oxygen. Her eyes bulged, blood red. She's choking, he thought.

Mitch scrambled up her naked body. He grabbed her lower jaw in his right hand and with his left pressed against her forehead. Her skin felt molten hot. He pulled her mouth open, and when he did, a thick, black tongue fell out.

"Oh, fuck!" he screamed. She was dying. She couldn't breathe, and she would die if he didn't help her.

He leaned in toward her, their faces inches apart. He closed his eyes and pressed his mouth against hers, the only bit of CPR he could remember.

When her black tongue entered his mouth, the taste of rotten meat was overwhelming. He felt his stomach flip and fought not to puke, but it was a losing battle, and he could feel the vomit rushing up his throat.

He went to pull back, to separate his mouth from hers, but before he could, she sank her teeth into his lips. The pain was worse than anything he'd ever felt. Even worse than when he jumped off a swing in third grade and tried to fly, breaking his left arm in the process.

Mitch shrieked in agony, but the rotting mouth pressed against his own muffled the screams. He felt the puke gush from his own mouth and into hers, then splash back against his bleeding lips, and he tried again to scream. That was when he woke up.

His heart beat so hard in his chest that he could have seen it if the room was illuminated, but it wasn't. He sat up fast and smacked his forehead against the bunk above him. Although it hurt like hell, it helped push away sleep and that horrible, revolting dream.

That's when he realized he could still hear screaming. He brought his hand to his mouth, thinking it was himself, but as he covered his own lips, the screams continued.

A red light flickered and danced on and off like a strobe in a night-club. In the crimson flashes, he could see the chaos in the room.

Two men held down a guard and ate intestines from an open wound in his midsection.

Dark.

A nurse chewed on the arm of a boy who Mitch had earlier seen crying about not getting lime Jello.

Dark.

A bearded man dragged another man from the top bunk and chomped into his throat.

Dark.

A naked woman with blood covering the entire front of her body sprinted a collision course toward Mitch.

Dark.

Mitch jumped out of his bed and backed away. The light came back on, and she was only feet away from him. He tripped over something and fell backward, landing hard on his bony ass, and the light went off again.

Someone grabbed him from behind and dragged him. Mitch flailed and struggled and his fist connected with something hard.

"Stop fighting, you shit!"

The voice was familiar. The light blinked back on, and Mitch saw it was Winebruner. He pulled Mitch toward the exit as the light went off again.

"What's going on?" Mitch asked.

"Shut the fuck up!"

The red light went off as they reached the glowing exit sign, and Winebruner swiped a card through the slot by the door. Mitch saw the bloody woman still running at them, but Winebruner kicked the door open and dragged Mitch through it.

The steel door slammed shut behind them, and they were in a puke green hallway. The woman hit the other side of the door, and they watched through the narrow slit of a glass window as she clawed and scratched. When that failed, she started smashing her head against it.

Mitch jumped to his feet. "Holy shit! They're zombies, aren't they? They're fucking zombies!"

Winebruner nodded. "I really thought those rumors were bullshit. But there's no denying it now."

The woman on the other side of the door had split her forehead open and bone showed through under the mangled skin.

Mitch looked back to Winebruner, who wasn't looking too hot himself. Even under the dim fluorescent lights, the young man looked haggard and his eyes had sunk deep into the sockets. Snot oozed from both nostrils, and when he saw Mitch looking, he hurriedly wiped it away.

"Do you know where our parents are?

"Supposed to be in E wing. But who knows now?"

After being shown to his bunk, Mitch was left with nothing to do but study an informational booklet on the bunker in which they were now housed. Built in the 1950s at the height of the Cold War, the bunker sat a few hundred yards under the Greenbriar Hotel. It could hold over two thousand people and survive a nuclear holocaust.

But what about zombies? That's the real test, Mitch thought. The book had included a map, which he'd reviewed over and over again in the intervening hours and had almost memorized. E Wing, if Mitch's memory was correct, was two lefts and four hallways from their current location.

"I think we should go there."

Winebruner looked skeptical. "What if there's more of them?"

The zombie at the door had now obliterated its entire face and nothing remained but bits of bone and sinew and two droopy eyes that dangled loosely from what had been their sockets.

"Well, we can't go back in there. What else should we do?"

"Wait. Or look for booze?"

"Yeah, let's not do that."

Mitch started up the hallway. When he got ten steps ahead, Winebruner followed.

They navigated the labyrinth of halls without making a single wrong turn. When they reached the steel door labeled simply "E," Mitch tried the door and found it locked.

"You need these to get anywhere."

Winebruner held up his key card.

"Where'd you get that, anyway?"

Winebruner flashed a shit-eating grin. "Lifted it from one of the guards. Being a delinquent brings with it a certain skill set."

Mitch nodded. He knew that all too well. "Well, do your thing, man."

Winebruner swiped the card, and, for a moment, the pinpoint LED light above the pad remained red. Then it flipped green, and Mitch pushed the door. It opened. He turned back and held the door for Winebruner, but when he did, he saw a zombie racing toward them.

Winebruner's back was to the creature, and he didn't see the soldier, all six and a half feet and two hundred and fifty pounds of it, approaching. He didn't see that the soldier's nose was gone, creating a black abyss in the middle of his bloody face. And he didn't see the soldier's throat was ripped out and blood from the gaping wound had turned his green uniform a dark, muddy brown.

But Mitch saw all of it. When Winebruner realized the boy was looking past him and not at him, he started to turn to see what Mitch was staring at. When he did, Mitch's hand darted out, and he snatched the key card away.

Winebruner looked down at his empty hand, like the straight half of a magic act trying to figure out what was going on, but he was too slow. Mitch gave him a hard shove in the center of his chest, and Wine-bruner stumbled backward.

He tried to regain his balance, but before he could, the soldier zombie was on him and snatched a handful of the delinquent's perfectly messy blond hair. Mitch hopped through the open door and swung it shut. As it closed, he saw Winebruner's eyes grow as big as ping-pong balls, staring at him as the zombie clawed at his cheeks.

Its fingers caught the inside of Winebruner's mouth and ripped away half of the man's face in one swift jerk. The zombie shoved the handful of shredded flesh into its greedy mouth and chewed it like it was prime rib. Even through the heavy metal door, Mitch could hear Winebruner's shrieking. He watched until the screams, and his pointless struggles, ceased.

"Nice knowing you, friend-o," Mitch said as he slid the key card into his pocket.

CHAPTER THIRTY-EIGHT

JULI WOKE DISORIENTED AND GROGGY. She looked to the nightstand, but the alarm clock was blank. The power had gone out around nine, she remembered. The night was black as molasses outside her bedroom window.

She was a sound sleeper and wasn't sure why she'd woken. She reached out and felt the other side of the bed with her fingertips. It was empty. Not just empty, but cool. Mark had gone to bed with her, but apparently, he'd been away long enough for his side of the bed to return to room temperature.

Her eyelids were getting heavy again, and Juli let them fall shut, but a crashing noise erased her sleep. She knew the sound the way a mother can recognize the crying of her own child in a sea of toddlers. It was the sound made by a dropped pan. Not just any pan. Venice Cookware. Juli squirmed out from under the sheets and fled the room.

She used the flashlight app on her cell phone to illuminate the way. The mahogany floor was cold under her bare feet and sent a little shiver up her back as she proceeded down the hall. She stepped in something moist and reached down to wipe the wetness from her foot. She held her fingers up and saw the tips were dark red.

Now, she ran down the hall and into the kitchen, where she saw her husband leaning over the sink, cradling his head.

"Mark? What's going on?"

He spun around and wiped something from his mouth. What was that smell? Vomit? Was Mark sick?

"Juli. Don't."

She didn't listen and kept coming toward him.

"Don't! Don't come over here!"

Juli slowed her pace but continued on. "What happened? Tell me right now, Mark!"

She approached the granite-topped island, above which her treasured cookware hung, and noticed an empty spot where her eight-inch omelet pan should have been.

"Mark?" She was panicked now. Why wasn't he answering her?

"Oh, God, Juli. I... I can't... Just don't."

Juli rounded the island, still watching Mark. She noticed a racquet-ball-sized wound on his naked shoulder. Before she could again ask what had happened, she followed his gaze, which he directed at the floor. There was something there.

No. There was someone there.

Juli aimed her phone at the shape on the floor and saw their daughter. Marcy laid motionless. Her caramel-colored hair was turning black, and a growing puddle of blood spread out around her head. The omelet pan laid on the floor a few feet away.

"Marcy!" Juli screamed.

She rushed to the girl and, in the process, stepped in the blood. Her feet flew out from under her, and she fell hard, catching her sternum on the island. There was a crackling sound like a wood knot popping in a campfire. Then she fell onto the slate floor.

"Don't," Mark said yet again.

"Stop saying that! Stop saying 'don't' and tell me what happened to our daughter!"

Juli crawled to Marcy on her knees, making trails through the blood. She rolled her daughter onto her back and saw the girl's temple was dented in like a discounted can of corn. She shook the girl, who remained motionless.

"Marcy, it's Mom! Wake up, Marcy! Marcy, wake up!"

She shook her harder, and the girl's head lolled back and forth. "Wake up! Just wake up!"

"She's dead," Mark said, his voice flat.

Juli's head snapped back as she glared at him. "What did you do!" It was an accusation, not a question.

Mark looked away at first, down at his feet. Then he glanced to his dead daughter. Then to his wife.

"She attacked me."

He didn't seem to realize it, but his fingers went to the red gash on his shoulder. "I came out for a pop, and I heard her in her bedroom coughing. But not really coughing. It sounded more like choking. So, I went to her room, and she was in the bed having a seizure."

He looked again at the body on the floor. Juli held her daughter's deformed head in her lap and stroked her wet, sticky hair.

"I ran to the bed and tried to hold her down so she wouldn't hurt herself, but almost right away, she stopped moving and stopped breathing. I tried to do CPR, but it didn't work."

"That doesn't make sense. Why is she in the kitchen? What happened to her head?"

Mark coughed and gagged. He turned back toward the sink but didn't make it quite in time and puke splashed over the counters. He retched a second time, then tried to compose himself.

"I left her room. I was going to get you. To call nine one one and tell you what happened, but when I started down the hall, I heard footsteps behind me. I thought it was Matt, but when I turned around, it was Marcy.

He turned back to Juli, and she'd never seen a look like that on his face before. It was fear and confusion and emptiness all wrapped together, and she shivered again.

"I grabbed her and hugged her and told her I was so happy because I thought she was dead, but then she bit me."

His hand went to his shoulder again, and Juli saw the wound looked like it might have been caused by teeth. But that couldn't be true. Marcy wouldn't bite someone. Who does that?

"I shoved her away, but she came right back, biting at me like an animal. So I pushed her away again and ran out here."

His eyes seemed to glaze over, and Juli thought he might cry. She'd only ever seen him cry once before, and that was when she told him she was going to leave him after she found the BJ video on his phone. He had cried like a baby then. But he didn't cry now. He just stared off into space.

"Mark? Tell me what happened."

"What?" He looked around the room, lost for a moment, then caught sight of his wife and dead daughter. "Oh. She got me again in the kitchen. She grabbed me and kept... biting..."

He stopped again. Sweat covered his forehead. "Biting..." he repeated as he scratched at the wound. His fingers dug into the red matter up to his knuckles.

"What are you doing? Stop it!"

Mark pulled at his skin, and the wound grew and ripped all the way to his nipple. "Bite."

His hand dropped away from the gash, and blood dripped onto the floor. He took a step toward his wife.

"Mark?"

He stopped walking and started running at her.

Juli screamed, and when he was less than a yard away, she pushed Marcy's corpse at him. His feet tripped over the body, and he did something akin to a pirouette before crashing into the counters and falling to the floor.

As he fell, Juli made it back to her feet, but they were still slick with Marcy's blood, and she slid on the slate floor like she was trying to walk on ice. She steadied herself against the island, and as she did, her hand brushed the cool grip of the butcher's knife. She'd asked Matt to put away the dishes, but he'd ignored her as usual. As her fingers closed around the handle, she was grateful for his carelessness.

Mark was back on his feet, snarling like a wild animal. Their daughter's blood was smeared across his face, which made his angry eyes seem downright insane, but Juli had no time to take it all in because he dove into her.

The force of his hundred and ninety pounds pinned her against the island, and her broken collarbone gave a sharp yelp for mercy. Spittle ran from his lips—he's foaming at the mouth, she thought—and his head struck at her like a snake. She pulled back and avoided his bite.

Juli held the knife in front of her as if Mark was a vampire she was trying to ward off and the knife was a crucifix. Mark dove at her again, and, this time, when he did, Juli aimed the blade and plunged it straight into his hungry, gaping mouth.

She felt his teeth shatter and break, and then the perfectly sharpened steel blade sliced through tissue and flesh. Mark's weight pushed the knife further into his skull, and when he landed atop of her, he was motionless. As his body slithered down her own and toward the floor, Juli gave the knife a hard twist, for Marcy.

She ran from the bodies of her dead husband and daughter and her fleeting moment of composure vanished as she remembered her only remaining family member. How was she going to explain this to Matt?

Juli sprinted up the steps toward the second floor, but halfway up the staircase, she heard a footfall. She couldn't let her son see his father and sister bloody and dead on the kitchen floor.

"Matt! Wait there, I'm coming."

But Matt's footsteps didn't stop. All Juli could think to say was 'Don't,' that stupid, meaningless word her husband had repeated, but she didn't want to say that, so she kept running until she hit the top step.

There she saw Matt. He was halfway up the long hall, which ended in his bedroom but also contained doors to the game room, half bath, and a linen closet. Matt fumbled with the knob to the closet like he'd never opened a door before.

"Matt?" He kept rattling the chrome handle. "Matthew?"

Juli had lost her phone somewhere in the kitchen and the only light in the hall was moonlight spilling through the overhead skylight. Matt was behind the light, immersed in the darkness.

"Matthew!" she yelled louder and shriller than she intended. That got Matt's attention. He dropped his hand from the doorknob and came to her.

It took three slow steps until he stepped into the light of the moon. As soon as that blue glow lit up his face, Juli saw the same blank nothingness that had overtaken her husband's once friendly gaze just before he attacked her. Her breath caught in her throat, and she felt so light-headed she might faint.

She wanted to faint. She wanted this to be a dream. And if it wasn't, she wanted to die. She'd thought losing her family's love was the worst thing to happen to her, but tonight was exponentially worse.

Matt passed through the moonlight and faded back into the abyss as he came toward Juli. Part of her, a large part, thought she should just let whatever was going to happen, happen. The only thing that snapped her out of that mindset was remembering Mark ripping his own skin off his chest and losing his humanity right before her eyes.

She didn't want to live. She wanted everything to be over so that she never had to think about this unimaginably awful night again. But she didn't want to be one of these monsters, either.

Matt was only a step away, and she could hear a deep, rattling groan spill from his slack jawed mouth. He clumsily swung at her, and Juli took a step back to avoid his hand. She turned and fled down the stairs, and, as she neared the front door, she heard Matt topple down them. She didn't look back.

Juli grabbed the keys to Marcy's Audi SUV off the stand in the foyer. Her own minivan was locked in the garage, but Marcy always parked in the drive. She ran into the night, and it was only when she felt the dewy grass under her feet that she realized she was still barefoot. Barefoot and wearing only a cream silk nightgown that just happened to be covered in blood.

Juli Villareal had a walk-in closet larger than most people's bedrooms and bursting with designer clothes, but she couldn't bear thinking about going back inside to get them. That life was over, and, as she remembered some old book title proclaiming, she could never go home again.

CHAPTER THIRTY-NINE

WIM SAT atop the gentle hillside that overlooked the farm when he heard the gunshots. From that vantage point, it all looked small and unimportant. He ran his fingers through the lush, green clover that covered the ground and which grew right up against the granite gravestones. One was for his parents, the other for his maternal grandparents. Both were simple, containing only their names, dates of birth and death, and "Beloved Mother" and "Beloved Father."

Wim always thought he'd be buried on that hill, too, presumably with a marker reading, "Beloved Son," but now he doubted that was true. He didn't even know if there was anyone left to bury him when his end came.

In the days after he cleaned out the town, he ventured into the surrounding farmland. He destroyed more than three additional zombies and hadn't found a single living person. He remembered an old movie with Vincent Price where he played a scientist left alone in a world overrun with vampires, and that's how he was feeling. Only the vampires were zombies, and he wasn't a doctor. And he knew he couldn't do this for years on end.

Wim pulled a handful of clover from the ground, spread them out in his palm and sorted through them.

"I wish you were here to tell me what to do. I never did like making decisions on my own."

All the clovers were of the three-leaf variety, and he dropped them back onto the ground. As he squeezed together another fistful, gunshots echoed in the distance. There were four in all, and they came from the north.

———

RAMEY AND STAN BARRELED DOWN A TWO-LANE HIGHWAY, WHICH WAS void of moving vehicles. Every few miles, they came across an abandoned car or truck, but they were easy to avoid. Stan had proved to be an excellent navigator as he kept them away from the cities but still moving toward the West Virginia star on Ramey's father's map.

They'd been on the road for about five hours when Ramey noticed Stan squirming in his seat and chewing his bottom lip like it was beef jerky. When he started squeezing his thighs together, her suspicions were confirmed.

"Need a bathroom break?"

Stan flashed a shy grin. "I've gotta piss like a racehorse."

Ramey pulled onto the curb. Trees lined the road on both sides. "The world is your toilet, Stan."

Stan hopped out of the truck and made a beeline for the cover of the woods. Ramey decided it was a good time to exercise her cramping calves. The truck was a beast, capable of going almost anywhere, but she had to stretch to reach the pedals, and now she was feeling it.

She bounced up and down on the pavement, shaking out the stiffness from her muscles and joints. Her stomach rumbled, and she realized she hadn't eaten all day. She also felt a tingling pressure in her own bladder and thought she might as well make full use of the stop.

"Hey, Stan, I'm gonna pop a squat, too!"

She headed to the trees on the opposite side of the road. There, she ducked behind a good-sized oak, dropped her pants, and did her business.

As Ramey zipped up, she heard the first gunshot. She didn't even button her jeans before running out of the woods. Two more shots thundered before she reached the road. When she broke clear of the trees, she saw two dead zombies lying across the dotted white line that divided the lanes. Then she saw Stan sprawled out on the pavement a few yards away.

A bearded zombie in a blue plaid shirt knelt over him and dined on his neck. Arterial blood spurted from the wound and dyed the zombie's gray beard scarlet.

Ramey passed the two fallen zombies. One had a hole in its cheek. The other a bullet wound in its chest and another through its left eye. Stan's silver pistol glinted in the sunlight a yard from where the lumberjack zombie was making him its lunch. Ramey had lost her appetite.

"Oh, Stan," she said as the zombie took an extra-large bite that ripped out the trucker's Adam's apple.

The zombie glanced back at her but didn't leave its meal. Ramey knelt down and picked up the gun. She could still feel Stan's warmth on the grip.

She'd never fired a revolver before, but she'd seen it happen often enough on TV, and she pulled back the hammer. She was only four yards away from the zombie but took her time as she aimed for the back of its head. She shot the gun, and the recoil was so strong and unexpected that the revolver flew out of her hands and clattered to the ground behind her. In front of her, the zombie dropped on top of Stan and didn't move.

She picked up the gun again and started for the truck when the world went out of focus, and she lost all the strength in her legs. She fell straight down on her behind and sat there in a fog.

———

WIM HAD THE WINDOWS ROLLED DOWN AS HE DROVE, SO THE FIFTH SHOT came through loud and clear. That one was close. He estimated within a mile, and sure enough, he soon came upon carnage on the roadway.

Four dead bodies laid on the gray asphalt. Nearby sat what his Mama had always called a redneck pickup truck. Not far away, a girl, who looked to be around twenty, sat Indian-style on the road.

When Wim stopped the Bronco and climbed out, he saw she was holding a revolver in her lap with the barrel aimed at her face. She stared at the gun like a snake that had been hypnotized by a flute, and she didn't react to Wim's presence until he spoke.

"You all right, Miss?"

Ramey snapped out of her daze and looked toward him. Wim saw she wasn't twenty-something. She might be close, but she still had the look of a high school girl, not a college adult. Not that he'd ever been to college himself. Her alabaster skin was almost void of color, which made her deep, chocolate-colored eyes stand out. Her pale, pink lips had a perfect Cupid's bow, and she opened her mouth but didn't say anything.

"Are you okay?"

Ramey blinked a few times, then looked back down at the gun.

"Why don't you give me that, Miss?"

Ramey's pretty eyes darkened with mistrust. "I think I'll hold on to it."

Wim took a step toward her. She pulled the gun closer to herself, but the barrel was still pointed in, not out, so he wasn't overly concerned.

"An empty revolver isn't of much use, but you do whatever you please."

Ramey looked into the barrel, squinted. "How do you know it's empty?"

"I heard four gunshots back at my farm. Heard another while driving." He pointed toward the gun. "My eyes aren't quite what they used to be, but that there looks like a Ruger Blackhawk, and they only hold five rounds."

She looked again at the gun. "Maybe I reloaded. Maybe I put in another bullet for myself."

Wim saw her eyes were ringed red. "Maybe you did. That would be a shame, though." He took slow, small steps toward her as he talked.

"Why?"

"'Cause up until ten minutes ago, I was thinking I was the only person left alive in the whole wide world. Now I know there's two of us. I'd hate to see that go back to one again."

Ramey wiped her eyes. "I killed my mom yesterday." Her face looked more alert than he'd seen so far. "Well, she killed herself. Then I killed her again."

Wim, who had loved his mother more than himself, more than anyone, couldn't imagine anything so horrible. He squatted down in front of the girl and saw she was on the verge of being beautiful. Probably would be already if the shell shock was gone.

"I'm real sorry to hear that."

Ramey nodded. "Thanks. Have you killed anyone?"

Wim's eyes broke free from her questioning gaze. "Yep." He didn't elaborate, and she didn't ask. "I have plenty of ammunition if you want."

Ramey handed over the revolver. "Okay."

Behind her, Wim spied a dead man in the road pushing another dead man off itself. The one moving had its throat ripped out, and Wim could see the exposed and partially eaten trachea. Its mouth gaped open.

Her back turned, Ramey saw none of this. That's for the best, Wim thought.

The zombie noticed them and shambled toward them.

"Why don't you go over to my Bronco and get a box of .45 shells. They're in the back seat. It'll be a yellow box, and they're marked."

Wim reached out, and she took his hand and let him help her to her feet. She was light as a feather and bounced a little when he pulled her up, and that made her smirk. He didn't see that because he looked past her to the zombie who used to be Stan, the truck driver.

Ramey moved by Wim on her way to his Bronco, and as soon as she was one step past him, he raised the Ruger and fired a round into the zombie's head. The bullet caught him on the right side of his forehead, and a small burst of blood shot out like water from a drinking fountain.

Ramey spun around in time to see Stan hit the ground. She looked from her former companion to Wim. "I thought you said it was empty."

Wim half-smiled. It felt good to smile. He couldn't remember the last time he had done so. "That might have been a fib."

"I'm gonna have to keep my eye on you." Ramey, to his surprise, smiled back. Fire had returned to her eyes, and along with it, some color to her face. "What's your name, anyway?"

"My name's Wim."

"What kind of name's 'Wim'?"

"Actually, it's William. But when I was little, I tended to mumble."

"You still do."

Wim could feel his cheeks heat up as a blush spread across them. "Anyway, when I told people my name, it came out more like 'Wim'. It stuck."

"Well, it's nice to meet you, Wim. I'm Ramey. Do you live around here?"

Wim nodded. "About eight miles back that way."

"I'll follow you?"

"I like that plan."

CHAPTER FORTY

IT WAS dark when Aben came to, and he was pleased to discover that he hadn't bled to death during his unintentional siesta. Part of him wondered if maybe he had died and didn't realize it. Do zombies know they're dead?

He looked at what used to be Dolan, and his stomach flip flopped. He had no desire to take a bite, and that convinced him he wasn't a zombie. He climbed to his feet, careful not to disturb his destroyed hand, and tucked the dead policeman's pistol into the waistband of his pants.

Aben vacated the police station, and as he stepped out into the night, the first thing he saw was a zombie stumbling up the street. It was an older woman, clad in a floral print housecoat that hung halfway between her knees and ankles. Her hair was rolled up in blue curlers.

More zombies filled the town. Some of them grouped together like packs of feral dogs, while others went the lone wolf route. Aben was careful to avoid all of them, but he took out the pistol just to be safe.

The more he moved, the more his hand ached. It was a throbbing fire that burned the whole way up his arm. He risked a glance at the bloody, mangled mess and knew it was only a matter of time before infection set in. If the situation in this town was an indication, a trip to the hospital was not an option.

Aben never believed much in fate, but when he saw a faded awning reading, "Clark's Hardware, Tools & More," he took it as an omen.

He used the grip of the pistol to knock out a pane of glass on the door to the shop. He scanned his surroundings to make sure none of the zombies heard, then reached through and opened the door and moved inside.

After browsing the store for a few minutes, Aben had gathered together a series of items he thought might be of use. A first aid kit, a table vice, a Bernzomatic gas torch, and a reciprocating saw. Thank God for battery-powered tools. Tinkering with the equipment kept his mind off what he was about to do, at least to some extent, but before long, everything was ready to go and it was time to focus.

Aben started off by using the vice to secure his ruined hand to the checkout counter. He tightened it down as hard as he could stand, then tried moving his arm. It didn't budge, and he was content that it would stay in place.

He loaded the reciprocating saw with a dual-purpose blade, one suited for cutting both wood and metal. They didn't make blades meant for cutting through bone, at least, not ones you could buy in the corner tool shop, but if this six-inch yellow blade could cut through steel, he didn't think his ulna and radius would put up too much of a fight. He had the torch close by and could only hope he didn't pass out before he could use it.

Aben squeezed down the trigger of the saw with his right hand, just to get a feel of it. It jerked like a son of a bitch, but it had enough weight that he felt gravity would work in his favor. He rested the blade about an inch above the cut on his wrist. He wondered if he should count to three, got to one, then went to town.

The pain as the saw cut through the layer of skin coating his arm wasn't as bad as he'd expected. It was fast and reminded him a little of a time he'd skinned his knee down to the bone playing wiffle ball in a church parking lot. But that only lasted two seconds. Then he was on to the hard part.

When the blade hit the white bone, his entire body shook. He worried that his arm would be jerked free from the vice and pressed down even harder. He felt the scorching heat as the friction turned the blade red hot. The pain he'd felt when his hand was degloved was a pinprick compared to the saw ripping through his radius. There was a moment of relief as the bone gave way, but the radius was next. *Why didn't I get drunk?*

He felt himself slipping away. Maybe it was the blood loss—it was coming out so fast—or maybe it was the pain. Either way, he tried to focus on the pain, which was worse than he ever could have imagined, but he latched onto it to keep himself conscious.

About half way through, the smell hit him. It was like burning hair combined with a sirloin steak cooked too long on a charcoal grill. He held his breath as he kept cutting. His good hand had gone numb from holding onto the vibrating saw, but he needed to finish while he could still hang on to it.

After what seemed like an eternity, he felt the radius bone splinter and break, and with the hard material out of the way, the blade ripped and tore through the remaining flesh in seconds. The saw tumbled from Aben's hand and crashed against the floor, where it petered out in a few dying chugs.

Even though he'd kept the belt tourniquet in place, blood still rushed from the site of the amputation. He grabbed the Bernzomatic. What an appropriate name. It sounded like something Ron Popeil would sell in a late night infomercial.

"Buy the Bernzomatic, and you can do your own at-home amputations!"

He pressed the button, and blue flamed roared from the nozzle. Aben gritted his teeth so hard he thought they might shatter as he held the fire to the bloody stump of his wrist and cauterized the wound. After ten seconds of fire, he turned it off and set the torch on the counter.

Aben was proud of himself for not passing out again. He expected to lose consciousness halfway through the cutting part and then bleed to death with his arm trapped in a vise. Then he'd come back as a zombie and spend eternity stuck to the table and unable to move more than a foot in either direction. That would suck even if he was dead.

He looked down at the black flesh of his arm, pleased with the results. He'd seen field amputations in Iraq that weren't much better. Aben dumped an entire bottle of peroxide over the wound, then wrapped it in gauze. He finished it up by securing the white gauze to his arm with duct tape. He was a man, after all.

Aben deposited various first aid supplies into a canvas bag which he then slung over his shoulder. He took an eight-pound hammer maul in his remaining hand and headed into the night.

CHAPTER FORTY-ONE

BOLIVAR AND PEDUTO FLED SOUTH, out of the city. They caught I-95, but by the time they got to Crum Lynne, a multi-vehicle pileup blocked the road, making it impassible. They abandoned the Smart Car and made their way on foot.

Peduto made several attempts to contact Sawyer via the radio to no avail. Neither of them said anything about that. Peduto then tried other bands, but the radios had gone silent. They were unsure whether that was intentional or a sign that things had taken a terrible turn.

Outside the Chester Prison, they ran up on a group of zombies eating a policeman, and when the zombies saw them, three of the creatures ditched the cop buffet and gave chase. Peduto shot two of them, and they lost the third after cutting through a park.

By this point, Peduto wheezed and struggled to keep up. They came across an abandoned Saab with the engine still running. A severed and chewed-upon arm rested on the seat, but the car had over half a tank of gas, and the situation didn't allow them to be choosy.

They caught Highway 13, where they drove as fast as they could. Only a handful of cars moved on the road, but plenty of abandoned vehicles littered the highway. Jorge noticed some of them contained undead passengers fighting to get out. Apparently, in death, fine motor skills like the type needed to open car door handles disappeared.

Random zombies roamed about, and a few of the fast ones gave chase to them as they passed by, but they soon lost interest when the Saab sped away. Jorge drove while Peduto rested. Her breaths were thick, and she kept clearing her throat of phlegm. Neither of them acknowledged that either.

Just before noon, they hit the section of 13 where it aligned with Interstate 495 and ran parallel to the Delaware River. South of Philly, there were a few more cars in motion, and when they got to 495, it had an almost normal amount of traffic moving in both directions. They hadn't seen any zombies in miles.

"Pull over for a few minutes," Peduto said, and Bolivar eased the car onto the berm.

She stepped out of the vehicle and stretched out the aches. She walked around the rear and took a seat atop the gray trunk as she looked north toward the city in the distance. Bolivar joined her.

At 11:58, jets roared overhead, but they weren't the kind carrying passengers into Philadelphia International. They were warplanes, A-10 Thunderbolts, and they were headed to the city.

Precisely at noon, the smoke came into view. Black masses of it billowed into the air in a way that reminded Bolivar of the footage of wildfires in California he saw on the news almost every year. Only there was nothing natural about this. The city of Philadelphia was burning, and whoever had still been alive when the fire rained down was incinerated.

He felt empty inside as the realization swept over him. He'd seen horrible, unbelievable things the last few days, but part of him still believed it could be reversed. But there was no coming back from this. Nothing could ever be the same again. He felt like he had a front-row seat to the end of the world.

"I'm sorry," Peduto said.

Bolivar noticed she was staring at him, not at the city. It was only then he realized his cheeks were wet with tears. He wiped them away with the back of his hand.

"It doesn't seem real, does it? None of this," he said.

She didn't respond. Instead, she slid off the trunk and got back into the car. Bolivar followed, and they drove on.

CHAPTER FORTY-TWO

WIM BUILT a fire in the stone pit outside his home and cooked them supper. Canned meat and veggies combined into a makeshift stew. The flames and the smell reminded him more than a little of burning the bodies of his acquaintances and neighbors in town, but constant chatter from Ramey helped take his mind off that part.

The girl was a talker, that was for sure. He thought it seemed her natural demeanor, but her rapid pace and sky-high inflection made him believe at least some of it was nerves.

She had an edge to her, one he suspected hadn't built up over just one day. But there were fleeting moments, like when she told him about getting an uncontrollable fit of laughter during her junior high Christmas pageant and her father laughing along in the audience where he could see the shell wasn't too thick.

He got most of her life story over the course of an afternoon and evening. She left out the part about Bobby Mack but didn't hold back on the rest. Ramey was candid about her mother's life and death and had just started on the subject of her father.

The wistfulness she used when speaking about him made the man seem almost heroic. Wim wondered how a man who could walk out on his family during a crisis was worthy of such admiration, but he listened and didn't judge, at least not out loud.

"He always thought I'd grow up to be a scientist like him, or maybe even a doctor. But even when he was around, I didn't want that life. Cooped up in a lab all the time, surrounded by all that sickness."

She shivered. The sun had set, and only the orange embers of the fire illuminated them. "Your log is closer to the fire than mine," Ramey said, and she used that as an excuse to sidle up next to him.

Her thigh brushed against his, and he almost scooted away. She was eighteen and an adult, or so she said, but all her talk of high school drama had made the years between them feel like a chasm. Nevertheless, as she leaned into him and rubbed her hands over her upper arms for warmth, he decided that sharing body heat was normal enough.

"I think it broke his heart when I wouldn't go with him. And I probably wanted to hurt him, at least a little, because I thought if he saw I wasn't leaving, maybe he'd stay, too. Stay for me. But he didn't." She fell silent for a little while, but that was okay. Wim didn't mind, and she never stayed quiet for long.

"I have to try to find my dad. I know it's ridiculous. And I know he's probably as dead as everyone else, but I need to know for sure."

Wim stared into the rust-colored coals and pondered this. He did think it was ridiculous. Ridiculous and needlessly dangerous, but who was he to crush whatever little hope she still had left?

"I understand. I do believe it's safer here, though. I've pretty near cleared the area of zombies. It wouldn't be a bad place to wait things out for a while. At least, until we see what happens."

"I know." She reached over and placed her small, soft hand atop his thick, calloused palm. "And I won't ask you to leave here. But I have to know. I have to go on."

Wim slid his hand free and took a hickory stick he'd been using as a poker and stirred the coals. They blazed crimson momentarily before fading back down. "All right. But stay in Mama's room tonight. The linens might be a little musty, but the bed's soft, and I suspect you need your rest."

She looked up at him and smiled. He felt gooseflesh prickle his forearms, and it wasn't because of the cool May air.

"I'll do that." Ramey stared at him for so long that he broke eye contact and looked away.

"Are you happy here, Wim?"

He didn't meet her gaze as he tried to answer the question, both to himself and aloud to her. "I was. I won't lie, it got lonesome at times, but that never bothered me all that much. Now..." His eyes drifted up, and he saw she still examined him. "I guess I'm not sure about a lot of things anymore. What made you ask?"

"I couldn't understand why someone like you is all alone in the world. I figured it must be by choice."

She covered her mouth to hide a yawn. "I think you're right about needing rest." Ramey stood and stretched, and he couldn't help but notice how the remaining light of the fire silhouetted her figure.

"Thank you, Wim, for saving my life and for bringing me into your home." She bent at the waist and gave him a soft kiss on his cheekbone, just below his right eye. "And for not letting me be all alone tonight."

He opened his mouth to say, 'You're welcome,' but before he could work out the words, she skipped toward the house.

He sat there for a long while and watched the fire wither, then die out completely. It occurred to him he'd spent more time talking to this girl he'd known for only a few hours than he'd spent talking to his neighbors in several years. It surprised him how much he enjoyed it.

Wim retreated to the house and checked the bedroom. The door hung half open, and he saw Ramey sprawled on the bed. She looked to have fallen asleep as soon as her head hit the pillow and hadn't even covered herself. Her breaths came out in soft puffs. Wim tiptoed into the room and took a blanket from the cedar chest. She didn't wake when he cloaked her in it.

In the morning, she was gone.

———

EVEN WITHOUT THE ROOSTERS AROUND TO COCK-A-DOODLE-DO, WIM woke before sunrise. Long habits were hard to break. He hadn't undressed the night before and didn't bother changing clothes. After he made his bed, he eased out of the room and into the hall.

The bedroom door hung ajar, and when he peeked inside, the bed was empty. The blanket he'd covered Ramey with the night before was folded neatly at the foot of the bed. It surprised him that the girl was up so early. He was also disappointed as he'd hoped to fix something passing for breakfast for her before she awoke.

He found the kitchen as empty as the bedroom, and when he looked out the window, he saw that his Bronco sat alone at the end of the dirt driveway. The only sign of her truck was some fresh tracks in the soft earth.

"Well. Damn."

He liked the girl. He enjoyed her silly stories and her sense of humor. But more than that, he liked her company, even if he'd only shared it for half a day. He also felt sick with worry. It was one thing being alone on the farm. It was another altogether being alone out there, on the road where any number of awful things could happen.

His appetite had disappeared, but he sat at the kitchen table until the sky transitioned from navy to robin's egg blue. Then he moved outside, where he saw a note tucked under the windshield wiper of his Bronco. There were only four lines of pretty, loopy script.

"Thank you again for everything and for understanding why I have to leave. I took a box of bullets. Now I know the gun can fit six."

She signed off with a lopsided heart and the letter 'R'.

Wim folded the note into fourths and slid it into his back pocket.

————

"I never expected this would happen, but I'm leaving the farm."

Wim sat facing his parents' tombstone. He'd gathered a clump of yellow tulips and held them in his hand. He looked from the silky petals to the grave, then back and forth again.

All morning long, doubt and worry filled him to the brim. He knew the opportunity to find Ramey had likely vanished. She'd shown him the map to her father's supposed residence, and he remembered the general location in southern West Virginia, but there were a dozen or more possible routes to get there.

At the same time, he knew nothing remained for him here. No farm. No animals. No town. And even though he frequently talked to his parents' headstones, they were long gone, too. Staying on the farm might be the safe choice, but it was a pointless one. A choice with no future. He was tired of simply existing. He needed to know what was happening in the world around him and if there was any point in going on.

Wim set the tulips in front of the marker and traced his fingers over the "Mother" engraving. "I'll miss you so much, but this is something I have to do. I know you'd understand, but that doesn't make it much easier."

Wim leaned in and kissed the tombstone. "I love you, Mama."

He left the only home he'd ever known and took nothing more than the guns, ammunition, and a small family photo album. He realized that with everyone dead, the album contained not only his memories but the only proof he and his family had ever existed.

Wim locked the front door behind him and resisted the urge to look back as he climbed into the Bronco and drove away. He turned left at the end of the driveway and headed down the empty, two-lane road.

"Goodbye," he said to himself because he had no one else to talk to. He hoped his days of being alone were nearing an end.

AUTHOR'S NOTE

If you enjoyed Hell on Earth (and I sure hope you did), please take a moment to leave a review on Amazon or Goodreads.

And, don't forget to check out the rest of the now completed series. ROAD OF THE DAMNED, THE ARK, I KILL THE DEAD and RED RUNS THE RIVER are all on sale now. Buy or borrow your copies on Amazon and see how the zombie apocalypse works out for our large cast of characters.

ROAD: http://www.amazon.com/dp/B01MUGBZ45

THE ARK: http://www.amazon.com/dp/B075WWD6BR

I KILL: https://www.amazon.com/dp/B078M6GN41

RED RUNS: https://www.amazon.com/dp/B07BPXSLVF

I'd also love for you to join my mailing list because, if you do, I'll send you 3 free short horror stories.

http://www.tonyurbanauthor.com/

And finally, feel free to add me on Facebook to read about my career, life, dogs, and adventures. http://facebook.com/tonyurban

ACKNOWLEDGMENTS

So many people lent me their advice and assistance as I wrote this novel. I'm sure I'll miss a few, but I want to thank the following:

Sharon Urban, my mother, for putting up with me during the year it took to write it and for being my biggest fan. She taught me to read, introduced me to horror, and turned me into the weirdo I am today. I owe her everything. Everything.

Nathan Faudree for providing invaluable advice and encouragement and being a source of endless inspiration to me over the years.

Jayne & Jan for reading and sharing their feedback.

Nathan G. for his expertise on airplane crashes, even if I ended up cutting those scenes from the book. Sorry!

All of the authors at 20BooksTo50K for helping me navigate the high seas of publishing.

And especially my good buddy Max Baldwin for ensuring that "Solomon" could curse like a proper Birmingham bastard.

ROAD OF THE DAMNED TEASER

Here's a Sneak Preview of "Road of the Damned", book 2 in the *Life of the Dead* series.

———

Juli thought what happened in her picture perfect suburban home was Hell, but that opinion changed when she reached the city. She'd planned to go to the police station and turn herself in. What exactly she would say was still something of a mystery, even though she'd been rehearsing it as she drove.

"Well, you see, officer, my husband murdered our daughter. Then he tried to murder me, but I killed him first. Then I went to check on my son and he was a zombie. No, officer, I'm not psychotic. No, I'm not taking hallucinogens. That's really what happened."

No one would believe that, of course. Juli herself barely believed it and she lived through it. Maybe she had lost her mind. In some ways, that might be for the best because she didn't know how she could live through what happened.

The night sky brightened as she neared the city, but it wasn't just the sea of streetlights that lit up the skyline as usual. Orange, shimmery smoke danced through the air like Baryshnikov, and the closer she came to the city, the brighter the night grew.

Even for a city, the streets seemed unusually occupied considering the time of night. People dashed aimlessly in every direction, carrying everything from TVs and stereos to toilet paper and jugs of water.

I'm driving straight into a riot, Juli thought. That there might be a correlation between the carnage in her home and the chaos in the city didn't even cross her mind.

A small teenage Asian boy ran past the front of her SUV, and if she'd have been going five MPH faster, she'd have hit him. She slammed on her brakes and he glanced back over his shoulder and mimed slitting his throat.

"Watch where you going, whore!"

You little punk she thought, but didn't say, not even behind the safety of her locked doors and windows. The teen ran off and she kept driving.

She saw a few people staggering about in a manner that reminded her of Mark, but tried to ignore them. That's not possible. They're old or hurt. That's all.

The smoke grew thicker as she closed in on a block of Government housing units. She saw smoke leaking from the windows in the upper floors, but there weren't any fire trucks on the scene. Instead, there stood a row of military vehicles. A few soldiers brandished big black guns as they stood guard outside the entryways. They stared at Juli as she passed by, but didn't move to stop her.

When she reached the next brick complex, she saw more soldiers, only instead of guns, they had tanks strapped to their backs. Juli thought they must be some sort of firefighters. When two black men ran out of the building, she quickly realized the soldiers weren't fighting the fires, they were starting them.

The soldiers spun toward the fleeing black men and aimed their nozzles. What came next was something Juli knew she'd never forget as long as she lived. From the nozzles gushed long sprays of fire, and the fire rained down on the two black men and coated their bodies in flames. They ran another ten feet, staggered and stumbled for five more, then fell to the ground, arms and legs flailing. Juli could hear their screams, which were high and strangely feminine, even with the windows up. The soldiers turned to her and waved her by. Nothing to see here. She drove on.

A few streets down, she reached a roadblock. A Dodge Charger police cruiser sat upside down on its roof. The siren blared. Dozens of people rocked it back and forth. Some had climbed onto the upside down undercarriage and jumped up and down, gleeful. Juli watched as several men dragged two police officers through the car's shattered windshield and into the streets where the crowd pummeled them.

Juli made a hard right into an alley. As her headlights lit up the narrow tunnel, she saw another police officer kneeling over a homeless man. When she neared them, she saw the officer's face buried in the man's belly. When the noise of the SUV got the cop's attention, it looked up and Juli saw blood and flesh dripping from its mouth.

She screamed and hit the gas. The SUV vaulted forward and bounced over the cop's legs. Juli checked the rear view mirror and saw it had returned to eating the bum. She was still looking behind her when she exited the alley and it was only the chorus of screams that drew her attention forward.

To her left, she saw row after row of police SWAT officers clad head to toe in black uniforms and body armor. Most held Plexiglas shields in front of them. As chunks of bricks, glass bottles, and assorted debris soared through the air, the need for them became clear.

To Juli's right were hundreds of residents of the city. Most were young and black, but several whites, Latinos, and Asians were mixed in. They held weapons of all kinds: guns, rifles, bats, shovels. They shouted at the police, and through the cacophony of voices, Juli heard their demands.

"Let us out! Let us out!"

"We have rights! You can't keep us here!"

"Fuck the pigs!"

Ragged coughs and sneezes rang out from both sides of the impasse.

The crowd of city dwellers moved forward. There were only twenty feet separating them from the police. Juli shut off the lights of the SUV and put it in reverse, letting it drift silently back into the cover of the alleyway. She stayed close enough to watch.

A teen ran to the front of the crowd and launched a forty-ounce beer bottle at the police. It somersaulted through the air and smashed into the face of a beefy cop who had picked the wrong time to look side-ways instead of straight ahead. He collapsed as if he'd been shot and two officers beside him raised their rifles, ready to shoot.

"Hold your fire! That's an order!" a blond-haired cop who tried to keep control screamed into a bullhorn. Then he turned toward the crowd. "There is a curfew in effect! Go back to your homes! You're safe there!"

"The fuck we are! Fucking pigs just want to make it easier to butcher us!" That came from a giant black man with a shaved head and bushy gray beard. He held a shotgun and he had it leveled at the rows of police. "We ain't stupid!"

The giant cocked the shotgun and held his finger to the trigger.

"Put down the weapon!" the cop in charge shouted.

The stand-off lasted maybe three seconds, but felt like a minute. Then the giant fired.

Birdshot slammed into police officers. Most received minor wounds, if injured at all, but one officer caught a BB in the eye and went to his knees holding his face. Blood seeped out from his fingers.

"Don't shoot! Hold your fire!"

One officer threw a can of tear gas into the rioters. Two more followed. Any chance of the stalemate ending peacefully went up in thick, yellow smoke.

Someone new shot. Juli couldn't tell which group fired first, but it didn't matter because more shots rang out in both directions. Bodies hit the ground on each side. Then the two groups raced toward each other. The battle was on.

Two teens beat a cop to death with baseball bats.

An officer with a rifle fired again and again and again, dropping half a dozen people in mere seconds.

Someone tossed Molotov cocktails and a trio of cops went up in flames.

A cop shot a boy in the throat. Then, as the boy lay dying in front of him, the cop put his pistol to his own temple and blew off the top half of his head.

After that, Juli saw a rioter who was sprawled prone on the ground as it was being chomped on by another protestor jump to its feet and run at the cops. It tackled an officer to the ground, then leaned in and ate away the cop's ear.

"Oh, dear God," Juli said to herself. She couldn't believe it was happening. She wished she'd have stayed in her house and died with her family. That would have been better than being out here with these monsters, with nowhere to go. Just waiting to be killed. Out here she was going to die alone.

The blond cop who'd been in charge tried to fight off another officer who had a knife sticking out of its throat. The blond cop beat it with the bullhorn, but two other zombies joined in. Juli could hear him shrieking as he was eaten alive.

Within minutes, at least half the crowd were members of the undead, and this new faction fought together to destroy the living. Cops attacked fellow cops. Rioters ate other rioters. So much blood flowed that Juli saw it gushing down the gutter and into the sewer grates.

She stared out at the carnage unfolding before her, frozen until a zombie slammed into the grill of her SUV. It was a female police officer, her ginger ponytail twisted askew under her riot helmet. Her throat was torn out and Juli could see gristly tendons and veins exposed. The zombie pulled itself up the hood and grabbed onto the windshield wiper. Its face pressed against the glass, smearing red splotches.

"Get off!" Juli yelled. She hit the wipers, which swished to and fro and dragged the zombie's arm back and forth in an undead wave. Juli smacked her hand against the inside of the windshield. "Get off!" she tried again, not sure why she was even saying the pointless, useless words out loud.

The zombie's face was even with hers and she looked into its dull, gray eyes. There was nothing alive left inside those eyes. It made her think of the eyes of a swordfish Mark had caught on one of their vacations to Key West and later had mounted to hang on the wall of his man cave. As Juli stared into the dead woman's eyes, the zombie's head bounced off the windshield. The skin on its forehead split and blood poured out. Then it smashed into the windshield again and its eyes closed.

Juli looked past it to see a black woman in her sixties holding a baseball bat. A bloody baseball bat. She wore her hair in tight cornrows and had thick, horn-rimmed glasses. Behind her was a boy in an

Orioles t-shirt. He held a rag against his head and had blood running down his face.

The woman scurried to the passenger side door and leaned close to the glass barrier.

"Let us in. Please."

Beyond them, Juli saw the street was overrun by zombies. They descended upon the few living people, who were attacked, eaten, and reanimated.

"I'm begging you! Please!"

Juli hit the unlock button and the woman jerked open the rear passenger door. She pushed the boy in first, then climbed in behind him.

"I'm Juli."

The woman peered at her through the gaps in the front seats.

"That's nice. Now, how about you get us the hell out of here."

Juli put the vehicle in reverse and backed up as quickly as she felt comfortable going between the narrow walls. In her mirror she saw the cop she'd earlier ran over. He crawled toward them, dragging himself along the pavement with his hands. The bum was now on his feet and sprinting toward them.

Juli hit the cop first. The bumper connected with his face with a hard smack. Then she hit the bum, who careened off the SUV, hit the wall, and bounced back into the path of the vehicle. The Audi bounced up and down, up and down, as the front and rear wheels rolled over him.

Juli glanced at the woman. "Sorry about that."

The woman shook her head. "Honey, you ain't got to apologize for nothing if you can get us out of the city."

"I'll do my best."

They exited the alley and Juli turned back in the direction from which she'd entered town. They passed by the same buildings, which were now fully engulfed in flames. Several burning zombies shambled along the streets. Two zombies, charred black like chicken after a grilling mishap, ate a soldier who still had a flame thrower strapped to his back.

"It's the end of days..." the woman whispered.

"What?"

She looked away from the death, to Juli. "Nothing. Don't mind me, Miss. I'm Helen." She patted the boy on his thigh. "And this is Jeremy. My grandson."

Jeremy didn't look up.

"What happened to him?"

Helen pulled Jeremy's hand off the rag on his cheek but the rag stuck fast. She peeled it away and it ripped like Velcro.

"Police whooped him a good one." She gently pressed down on a bloody wound on the boy's cheek. Juli thought she could see bone underneath it. He let his head rest against the window and took shallow, ragged breaths.

"Should we go to a hospital? For help?"

Helen stared out the window to the city that was falling around them. "No... No, honey. I do believe we're on our own, now."

As Juli drove on, she realized the old woman was correct.

Made in the USA
Middletown, DE
23 July 2023

35634652R00163